LONGWALKER'S JOURNEY

A Novel of the Choctaw Trail of Tears

LONGWALKER'S JOURNEY

BEATRICE O. HARRELL

Illustrated by Tony Meers

DIAL BOOKS FOR YOUNG READERS NEW YORK

Published by Dial Books for Young Readers
A division of Penguin Putnam Inc.
345 Hudson Street
New York, New York 10014

Library of Congress Cataloging in Publication Data
Harrell, Beatrice Orcutt.
Longwalker's journey: a novel of the Choctaw trail of tears/
by Beatrice O. Harrell; illustrated by Tony Meers.—1st ed.
p.   cm.
Summary: When the government removes their tribe from their
sacred homeland in 1831, ten-year-old Minko and his father endure
terrible hardships on their journey from Mississippi to Oklahoma,
where Minko receives the name Longwalker.
ISBN 0-8037-2380-6 (trade)
1. Longwalker—Juvenile fiction. [1. Longwalker—Fiction. 2. Choctaw
Indians—Fiction. 3. Indians of North America—Fiction. 4. Frontier
and pioneer life—Fiction.] I. Meers, Tony, ill. II. Title.
PZ7.H2347Lo   1999
[Fic]—dc21   98-9754   CIP   AC

*This book is dedicated to my friend, mentor,
and fellow Okie, Charles "Chuck" Sasser,
who encouraged me to write
and believed I might be good at it.*
—B. O. H.

To my parents.
—T. M.

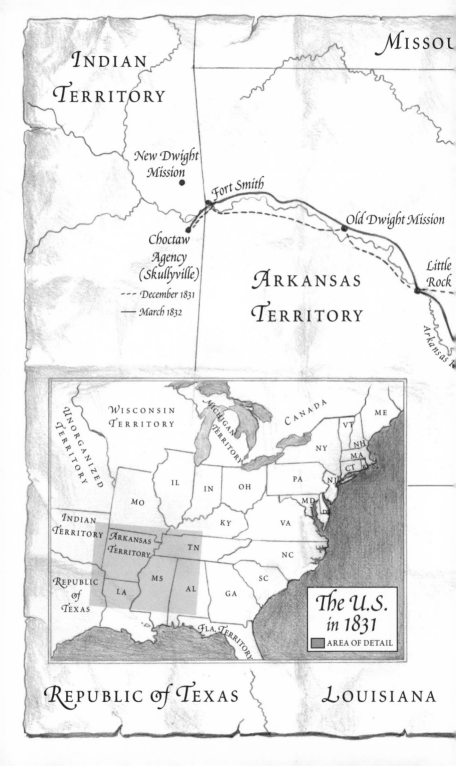

INDIAN TERRITORY

MISSOU[RI]

New Dwight Mission

Fort Smith

Choctaw Agency (Skullyville)

--- December 1831
— March 1832

Old Dwight Mission

Little Rock

ARKANSAS TERRITORY

Arkansas R[iver]

REPUBLIC OF TEXAS

LOUISIANA

UNORGANIZED TERRITORY

WISCONSIN TERRITORY

MICHIGAN TERRITORY

CANADA

ME

VT

NH

NY

MA
CT R[I]

NJ

IL

IN

OH

PA

MO

MD

DE

INDIAN TERRITORY

ARKANSAS TERRITORY

KY

VA

TN

NC

REPUBLIC of TEXAS

LA

MS

AL

SC

GA

FLA. TERRITORY

The U.S. in 1831

AREA OF DETAIL

A Note on the Old Choctaw Calendar

In this book I have used the names of the months of the year as they would have been used in the old Choctaw way, which differs greatly from the placement of the modern Choctaw month names. In the "old calendar," the year, which began with the first frost, was 364 days long. It was divided into thirteen months of twenty-eight days each, with the new month beginning on the first night of the full moon.

The old Choctaw month names used in this story correspond roughly with the following English months:

Hvsh Hopóni (Month of Cooking)
began around mid- to late September

Hvsh Chvfó Chitó (Month of Big Hunger)
began around mid- to late January

Hvshi Máhli (Wind Month)
began around late February/early March

Hvsh Bíssa (Month of the Blackberry)
began around late March/early April

Hvshi Bíhi (Mulberry Month)
began around late April/early May

Hvsh Tákkon (Month of the Peach)
began around late May/early June

PART

I

October 7–October 25, 1831

Chapter One

The dreaded day had finally come. Even now, the wagons were rolling into Minko Ushi's village on the Pearl River. His people, the Choctaws, were being removed from their sacred homeland to a place called Indian Territory. The westward journey was said to take three moons. The people did not want to go, but their homes and farms were being sold to the many white settlers who came in increasing numbers, hungry for land.

As Minko Ushi and his mother and father prepared to leave their farm, sadness crept on silent feet into the small cabin. He had heard his mother, Ulla Achufa Tok, crying in the night, but now she was busy with her tasks. Her waist-length black hair was neatly held in a single braid, and her soft deerskin dress came just to her knees. While some of the other women in the village had copied the frilly, aproned dresses of the

French women they had seen, his mother had refused to wear the fussy, confining clothes. Minko Ushi thought she looked beautiful in her simple dress as she went about the business of filling the flour sacks with dried corn and dried deer meat. She might have been getting ready for one of their many trips to the village of their relatives. This time, though, they would not be coming back.

Itilakna, Minko Ushi's father, had carefully explained that a chief called President Jackson in a faraway place called Washington had ordered all Choctaws to leave their homes.

Minko Ushi had not understood how this could be. "He is chief of the whites, Father. Why must the Chata obey him?" he had asked.

"Because he commands many soldiers, and if we do not obey, he will send them to kill us," Itilakna had said quietly.

Itilakna had been talking to Minko Ushi about the journey for days, but now, while the big government wagons rumbled into their village to take them away, Minko had more questions. "Will all of our people be leaving this day?" he asked.

"No, Son. The three districts—the Northwestern, Southern, and our own Northeastern District—have been separated into three groups. With each dying of the grass, another group will make the journey. Some of the people of the Northwestern District have already begun the move. But once all the Chata are removed from this place the whites call Mississippi, I am certain all the other tribes will be sent to Indian Territory too, because they have land for the taking."

"Why must they have my pony? He is small and not worth very much."

"I have already told you, Minko. Everything had to be sold, and what remains must be left behind. We may take only what we can carry."

"It is not right, Father. It is just not right," Minko Ushi said angrily. But his father only walked away, refusing to discuss what he had already explained many times before today. So Minko tried once more to talk to his mother about taking the pony along.

"Black Spot will be no trouble, Mother. I will take care of him. He belongs to me. He does not like strangers."

"We have talked about this enough, Minko Ushi. Your father has explained it to you. Black Spot is no longer yours. He belongs to the people who will live in this house after we are gone." His mother spoke softly and did not look at him.

Minko Ushi could feel her sadness, and he understood, because he also felt sorrow at having to leave, but he could not help feeling some excitement at the coming adventure. In all of his ten summers, he had never been farther away from home than his relatives' village, a two-day walk to the south. He could not imagine traveling as far as Indian Territory. If only he could take Black Spot, it would not be so bad to leave his home.

Before Minko Ushi could try once more to plead his case, his father appeared in the doorway of the little cabin. Itilakna was a big, powerful man with gentle brown eyes and a ready smile. He did not smile now but looked at his wife with concern.

"You look tired, Ulla Achufa Tok. Are you well?"

"I am well," she said, "but I fear this journey is going to be hard on all of us, especially Minko Ushi and the elders."

"We have all faced many hardships and survived them, just

as we will survive this. It will be hard for the elders, but they too are survivors. Minko Ushi is strong, and he will be fine. Is that not so?" he asked, smiling fondly at his son.

Minko Ushi smiled back at his father. "I am not afraid of the journey, Father, but I cannot leave Black Spot. He is my friend, and he must come with us."

"I wish he could, my son, but he cannot. Come now. We must go, the wagons are here."

They stepped out into the bright autumn day, and Minko Ushi stared at the ten big army wagons, drawn by teams of four oxen each, moving slowly toward a place just outside the village. Four hundred of the Northeastern District's three thousand people had been gathering there for several days, and now they watched silently as the canvas-covered wagons came to a stop. Minko Ushi saw that the men driving the wagons were civilians, while the many men on horses wore soldiers' uniforms.

A short, barrel-chested man with fiery red hair on his head and face climbed up on a wagon seat and began speaking in English. "I'm Wagon Master Timmons. We'll be loadin' the wagons now, so step lively." When no one moved, he began to shout. "All right, you people! I ain't got all day. We got to be in Memphis in three weeks, so let's move it. Anyone's too old, sick, or too young to walk, load 'em up. One other person can ride, to look after 'em."

Minko Ushi understood most of what the redheaded man said, because Itilakna was teaching him English. Many years of trading with the whites had forced Itilakna to learn their language. He shared his knowledge with his wife and son, and anyone else who cared to learn.

Many Choctaws understood English, though not many spoke it. Those who did not understand Wagon Master Timmons's words looked to their friends or relatives for translation.

Minko Ushi felt very proud when his grandmother asked him what the noisy white man was shouting about. "He says only the old and young and those who are sick may ride, Grandmother. And one to watch over them."

The gray braid hanging down her back swayed as the tiny old woman shook her walking stick in the general direction of the wagon master. She walked away muttering to herself.

Slowly the people began to climb into the wagons. Minko Ushi noticed that a small circle of women sat on the ground, their blankets over their heads, crying and wailing. Their husbands stood helplessly by, not knowing what to do, as the wagon master continued to yell at the bewildered Choctaws.

Minko Ushi's mother and several of the other women went to those who were crying and spoke softly to them. After a few minutes the women stood up and began touching the trees with both hands as the tears streamed down their faces. They were saying good-bye to their homeland.

Minko Ushi watched for a moment, then looked away. It made him sad, and he did not like the feeling. That's when he saw his little white pony with the black circle around one eye. He came trotting down the bumpy road behind the line of wagons. How had he gotten out of his pen? Minko wondered.

Well, no matter. It was surely a sign that his pony was meant to come with them. He closed his eyes tightly and asked the

Great Spirit to make Black Spot invisible until they got to Indian Territory.

His mother looked back at their home one last time, and Minko Ushi saw her bite her lip as the tears escaped her eyes. He watched his mother carefully, trying to tell if she had seen the pony. Sure enough, a little smile lifted the corners of her mouth. She looked toward her husband and lifted her chin in the direction of the pony, and in that mysterious way grown-ups have, Itilakna saw and understood her.

He was helping his elderly grandfather into the last wagon. Once that was done, he turned his attention to the little pony. "Go back, you silly horse, go back," he yelled, picking up stones to throw.

Minko Ushi ran to his father. "You see? Black Spot will not stay here alone," he said. "He knows his place is with me."

Black Spot stopped in the middle of the road, watching as Itilakna came closer. The stones flew through the air and landed in front of him. When Minko Ushi was sure the next stone would hit the pony, Black Spot wheeled around and ran back the way he had come. He disappeared around a crook in the road, and Itilakna returned to his family.

Minko Ushi felt the tears coming and fought them back. Choctaw boys did not cry, no matter how much they might want to. He looked sadly down the road and wished he were grown. Then he and Black Spot could make the journey together.

Mother climbed into the wagon with Itilakna's elderly grandparents, who were called Grandfather and Grandmother by everyone in Minko's family. She would ride with them because

there was no one else to do it. Most of Grandfather's family, including Itilakna's father and mother, had died in a raging cholera epidemic three years before, in the Northwestern District.

Once the wagons were loaded the order was given to move out. Minko Ushi heard the whips crack, and the heavy wagons creaked forward. The men, women, and children who would be making the journey on foot fell in behind the last wagon. The march had begun.

It was Hvsh Hopóni, the Month of Cooking, when the people should be cooking and drying their harvested crop. It seemed strange to Minko Ushi not to be carrying wood and laying out the corn for drying. Hvsh Hopóni, and the coming of cool weather, was always a happy time for the people. He did not like to see them walking along so silently. As the big wagons rolled slowly down the road and into the shaded forest, even the children were quiet.

For miles Itilakna and his son walked beside the wagons, saying very little. Minko Ushi finally grew tired of the silence and ran ahead to see if any of the other boys might want to play. He cut between the slow-moving wagons and had run only a little way when he saw a squirrel, who seemed to be watching the travelers from the safety of the trees.

Darting into the woods, Minko Ushi chased the squirrel until it disappeared into the deep shade. He stopped and began looking around for the wily squirrel. He was stooping over, inspecting a hole in the base of a big oak tree, when someone pushed him from behind. He lost his balance and fell over.

Minko Ushi jumped up, spun around, and prepared to do battle. And there was Black Spot, grinning at him. Minko Ushi laughed out loud and threw his arms around the little pony. "How did you get here?" he asked, then laughed again when Black Spot looked as if he were trying to answer.

"This will not do, Minko Ushi," said a voice from behind him. "You know you must not leave the group. It is too dangerous. And that horse must go back."

"But, Father, he has come so far. . . ."

Itilakna held his hand up, signaling for quiet. "You can get the family into a great deal of trouble if they think we are trying to steal this horse. They will say we are thieves, and they will not hesitate to kill us, Minko Ushi." He slapped the pony on the flank and shouted, "Run away, horse. Run. Go!"

The pony wheeled around on flying hooves and fled before the angry man's harsh words. Minko Ushi watched the pony disappear without saying another word.

Chapter Two

They were walking back toward the wagon when they heard gunfire. Itilakna started running, and Minko Ushi was right beside him. What if the soldiers had seen the pony and were, even now, killing his mother and grandparents to punish him? His heart was pounding, and he ran faster than he had ever run before. Onto the trail and down to the wagons they ran.

Soldiers were everywhere, waving their guns and yelling, "Back in the wagons! Back in the wagons, or we'll shoot!" Men, women, and children were scrambling to get back into the halted wagons, but the soldiers kept firing their guns into the air and shouting. When they reached their wagon, and Minko Ushi saw that his family was not harmed, his heart stopped beating so fast and he was able to breathe again.

"Some of the children and their parents got out of the wagons. The soldiers thought they were trying to go back home. They stopped the wagons and began shooting into the air." Mother spoke quietly, but her dark eyes flashed with anger.

"They do not want any Chatas to slip away and return home, so we will be watched until we are out of Mississippi," Itilakna said angrily.

With order restored, the wagons rolled slowly forward once more.

When the sun slipped out of the sky, the wagon train stopped and the people spent their first night on the trail. Campfires were lit, and family and clan members checked on one another to see that all was well. Mother's parents were allowed to go and sit at the fire of their daughter's camp, and they talked far into the night. Minko Ushi slipped into sleep, listening to the grandfathers' voices tell the old stories of times past.

At dawn they broke camp and climbed into the wagons once again. Minko Ushi was quiet as he walked along, thinking about Black Spot and wondering what the days ahead would bring. At midday the soldiers stopped, but only for one hour. While the people rested, the soldiers pulled back the canvas from the tops of the wagons. It was too hot inside and the riders were complaining.

Jerky was passed out to the people, because there would be no time to cook.

"You can eat when we stop for the night. We're behind schedule. Wouldn't want you injuns to miss the boat," laughed the red-bearded wagon master. The people continued to eat and talk quietly to one another. They seemed not to have heard

Timmons, and Minko Ushi smiled to himself as he watched the wagon master stomp away.

When they were moving once more, Minko rode in the wagon for a while with his mother and the grandparents. He chewed on the meat and looked at the passing scenery. He was now farther from home than he had ever been, but the land looked much the same. They were headed for a place called Memphis, where boats were to take them down the Mississippi River to Arkansas Territory. From there, the plan called for a stop at Arkansas Post, a small military outpost near the mouth of the Arkansas River, and then on up the Arkansas River to Little Rock and Fort Smith.

The people walked for twelve monotonous, weary days. Wagon Master Timmons grew more impatient as the days passed, and he fell farther behind schedule. The stops became shorter, and they began traveling for several hours after darkness fell. It was on one of these dark nights that Minko Ushi began to notice silent black shapes just inside the dark line of trees. He had to strain his eyes to keep the shapes in focus, but there seemed to be four ghostly shadows drifting along with the wagons.

He moved closer to his father but said nothing. They had been walking since sunup with only two short breaks, and everyone was exhausted.

When they finally stopped, the people were too tired to build fires, so they ate jerky and then wrapped themselves in their blankets and fell into sleep. Mother came to sleep with her little family, leaving the wagon to the children and elders.

Lying between his parents, Minko Ushi could still make

out the shadows by the trees. He waited until his mother was breathing deeply, then whispered, "Father? Are you sleeping?"

"No, Minko. What is it?"

"*Koi,* I think. The wildcats. They have been following us for some time."

"Where?" Itilakna asked quietly.

Minko Ushi pointed in the direction of the faintly glowing yellow eyes. "Will you tell the soldiers, Father?"

"No, Son. There is plenty of food for *koi*, so I do not think they mean us any harm. The soldiers would just kill them, and there is no need for that."

"Maybe they will come with us to Indian Territory."

Itilakna chuckled in the dark. "I think they are just curious. Sometimes when we go out to hunt, *koi* follow along, just out of sight."

"Mother says they are dangerous. They steal little children and eat them, she says."

"When times are bad and food is hard to find, they have been known to take small children, but you are safe, my son, because you are too big to carry off."

"Oh, I am not afraid. Not at all. I just thought you should know they were out there," Minko Ushi said quickly.

"You did the right thing, Son. I know you are not afraid, but it is good to respect your enemy."

"Good night, Father."

"Sleep well, Son."

In the chilly hours of dawn, the camp moved out. Minko Ushi looked for the big cats, but they had vanished with the night.

"Come on, you people. Git your lazy selves movin'," shouted Wagon Master Timmons from atop his prancing brown horse. The wagon drivers flicked their whips over the heads of the struggling oxen, and the wagons moved a little faster. Those who followed the last wagon soon fell behind, stringing out along the dusty trail. Wagon Master Timmons went to tie his horse to the last wagon. When he saw the walkers so far behind, his face turned as red as his hair. He snatched the whip out of the driver's hand, wheeled his horse around, and started back along the trail. He cracked the whip over the heads of the straggling walkers, hitting several people in the face.

The women picked up their children and began to run. The children were screaming and crying as their mothers stumbled and fell, and rose to run again. In a matter of seconds, Choctaw men surrounded the wagon master's horse. Terrified by the press of human bodies, the horse reared up on its hind legs and pawed the air with deadly hooves. One of the young men couldn't get out of the way, and the slashing hooves struck him in the head. Hands reached out to pull him away. The men laid him down gently, and Minko Ushi stared at the blood that flowed from the stricken man's head and stained the ground a bright red.

"No!" screamed the young man's mother, fighting her way through the ever-widening circle of people. Falling to her knees, she lifted her son's head into her lap. Moaning softly, she whispered, "No, my son. No. Do not leave me."

Wagon Master Timmons paid no heed to the fallen man. Roaring with rage, he cracked the whip into the crowd of people. The frightened horse continued to rear and kick its legs, but now the Choctaw men were rushing in to unseat the wagon master, fearless in their anger.

Itilakna had stayed with Minko Ushi during the commotion. Now he said, "Stay here, Minko," in a tone that tolerated no questions, and started for the circle of people. He had not taken more than two steps when the soldiers came, firing their guns over the heads of the Choctaw men. Itilakna went back to stand beside his son, putting a protective arm around his shoulders.

"You men move away from the horse," the young army captain shouted, in very poor Choctaw. "Move away, I say."

Reluctantly, the men moved away from the still screaming, red-faced wagon master. "I'll kill every one of ya godless heathens," he yelled. "The government shoulda killed ya all when they had the chance and saved us all this grief."

"That is quite enough, Mr. Timmons," the captain said. "You are hereby removed from your post as wagon master. Pack your gear and report to the removal agent in Memphis to collect your pay."

The wagon master went suddenly quiet, staring at the young captain in astonishment. "You got no authority to do this, Cap'n. None at all."

"You will remove yourself from my sight, Mr. Timmons, before I lose patience and do something we will both regret," the captain said through clenched teeth.

"Takin' the side of these red dogs against a white man, are ya?" Timmons was yelling again, raising his arm to unleash the whip. He never saw the two soldiers who walked up on the other side of the horse and pulled him to the ground.

"You ain't heard the last of me, ya traitor. Hear that, Cap'n?" Timmons shouted, as the soldiers took him away.

Calling for an interpreter, the captain asked the mother of the fallen young man if she would allow one of the soldiers to help her son.

"No one can help him now," she whispered. "He goes to join his ancestors."

The Long Walk had claimed its first life.

Chapter Three

When they were three days' walk from Memphis, the weather turned colder and the rain began—icy rain from which there was no shelter. Minko Ushi sometimes rode with his mother to escape the freezing downpour. The other walkers had no choice but to struggle on. The new dirt roads turned into rivers of mud, and the heavy wagons only added to the soggy mess. They made little progress, and finally on the second day the lead wagons sank in mud up to their axles and could not move. The shivering walkers left the trail to gather beneath the trees, and the soldiers let them go.

"Why are the soldiers using these muddy trails, Father? Do they not know there are trails through the forest that can be traveled when it rains?"

"They have been building new trails and repairing old ones ever since Jackson was chosen as their new chief. I think they will use these trails because it is their plan to do so, and they will not change that plan, no matter how difficult it becomes," Itilakna said with the ghost of a smile.

The captain went down the line of wagons and, speaking through an interpreter, told the Choctaws what must be done. "We will have to move everyone out of the wagons. The supply master will use the canvas covers to put up shelters. Any help you men can offer would be greatly appreciated."

Minko Ushi and his father helped the grandparents out of the wagon and to the cover of the trees while the soldiers struggled to remove the canvas from the big wagons. Once his grandparents were attended to, Itilakna went to see if he could help put up the shelters. Minko stayed behind to help his mother make the elders as comfortable as possible.

The corners of the canvas were lashed to the trees, and makeshift shelters were set up. Even though the ground was wet, the shelters were welcome, and once everyone was gathered beneath them, the captain came to speak to the people.

"The roads must be stabilized," he said. "The only way we can do that is to lay logs down every few feet or so. The wagon drivers and my men are working to cut trees down, but we need to get the trees from the woods up here to the road. We are asking your help to get this done."

The Choctaw people listened carefully and whispered among themselves when the captain had finished speaking. Minko Ushi moved among them, listening to what they were saying.

"If we do not help them, maybe they will let us go home," said a young woman as she shifted her child from one hip to the other.

"I will not help them move us away from our home," said a

young man who had almost been hit by the hooves of the wagon master's horse.

"We did not ask to be here," said an ancient old man. "Let them do their own dirty work."

When no one answered him, the captain left them, saying, "I will leave you to discuss this among yourselves." He started to walk away, then turned around. "But know this," he said. "We will continue on to Memphis, no matter how long it takes."

When he was gone, everyone started talking at once. Only two members of the tribal council were present. They took it upon themselves to demand quiet so that all who wanted to speak could be heard. In the ancient, time-honored way, every man and woman was allowed to speak his or her mind, and no one spoke in favor of helping the soldiers.

Itilakna waited until all the others who wanted to speak had been heard, and then he stepped forward into the circle.

"I know that none of you wish to help the soldiers, and while I agree with all that you have said, still I must ask you to think again." When the quiet rumble of disagreement stopped, Itilakna continued. "We have children and elders to think of. You know that we cannot go back. Our homes are gone. We must go forward, and the longer it takes, the more the defenseless among us will suffer."

"Do you say that we must help them, Itilakna?" asked an old woman, wagging her finger at him.

"I say that we must help ourselves, Grandmother. If we do not, there are those among us who will die here." He stood before them, waiting, as they discussed his reasoning.

Reluctantly, after much talk, they decided that they would help themselves and the soldiers.

"I do not like this, Itilakna," said the old grandmother, shaking her finger at him again, "and your grandfather will hear of it." Minko Ushi smiled to himself to hear someone speak to his father as if he were a child. Sometimes it was good to have the elders nearby.

So it was that 250 Choctaw men, young and old, and 22 young women cut and carried logs from the woods to the road. The soldiers dug trenches in the cold mud, and the logs were laid along a five-mile stretch of the new road to a place where the roadbed was on solid rock.

Mother forbade Minko Ushi to go into the woods because she had heard about the wildcats. All the other children were also cautioned to stay out of the woods.

"But, Mother, I am too big to be carried off by *koi*. Father said so."

"You will do as I say, Minko Ushi," Mother said, in a tone that allowed for no argument. "I do not think you will be carried off, but if you wander into the place of the *koi*, they will attack you, for they have young to protect."

"I should not have told that Turtle Clan boy about the *koi*. He went straight to his mother, and now all the mothers know," Minko Ushi said disgustedly.

Soldiers, civilians, and Choctaws worked in shifts through the night to get the wagons moving again. Just after daylight the work was done, and the exhausted people and the wagons began moving again. The rain continued to fall, sometimes a light mist, sometimes pouring out of the sky in a flood, but they walked on. Late that night, they made camp on high, rocky ground.

Minko Ushi had been watching for the wildcats, and at last, when the people broke camp at dawn, there the cats were, barely visible among the trees.

"They have come to say good-bye," Itilakna said quietly to his son. The Choctaws watched silently as the big cats slowly faded into the mist and were gone. With great sadness, the people walked toward Memphis and away from the old life, leaving only the great cats to remember what had been.

Tired, cold, and hungry, they arrived at the gathering place outside Memphis after eighteen miserable days of walking. The removal agent met them with more bad news.

Standing in the downpour in his rain slicker and muddy boots, he looked at the hundreds of brown faces and said, "There are no boats to take you down the river, and there are not enough tents for everyone, and we will have to ration the food." He lifted his hands in a gesture of apology. "I did not expect the army to delay in sending us the boats. We made no provisions for feeding and sheltering so many of you. I have sent for tents and food, but it may be a week or two before they get here. I don't know when the boats will come, either, so you may expect to be here for a while."

Minko Ushi was listening to the removal agent, but he was watching his father's face. He saw Itilakna's jawline tighten, and he knew that the anger was about to spill over.

Ulla Achufa Tok touched her husband's arm gently, and that invisible magic drew Itilakna away to walk and talk with her in whispers.

Late that night as Minko Ushi lay in the crowded tent, which leaked icy rain, he knew that he should be grateful his father had found friends who were lucky enough to get space in one of the few tents the agent could provide. Those friends had offered to share their tiny space in the tent. But he did not feel grateful. He felt like crying. He needed to get outside and breathe some cold air, or he would cry for sure. Quietly he picked his way through the sleeping people and stepped out into the frosty air.

The rain had slowed, but the night was eerily dark, for there were no campfires and no stars or moon. The cold air made him feel better, and he walked through the slippery mud to look for the wagon his mother and great-grandparents slept in. He knew that his mother would be sleeping sitting up so that the elders and the children could lie on the wagon floor. He also knew it was too crowded for him in there, but he wanted to go to her all the same.

After a few minutes of searching without finding the wagon, he sighed deeply and turned to go back to the tent. He had taken only a few steps when he heard a sound that made him freeze in his tracks. Something was moving toward him out of the dark, cutting him off from the tent. Eyes glowed red. If it was *koi*, it was huge.

It came at him so rapidly, he had no chance to react. The impact knocked him off his feet into the freezing mud. He had no weapon, so he prepared to use his hands and arms to defend himself. What he grabbed was wet and warm, and smelled like a horse. Black Spot!

The little pony stood over his owner, pawing the ground and shaking his mane. Minko Ushi scrambled to his feet and threw his arms around Black Spot's neck. He felt the tears running down his face, but he didn't care. All the sadness, anger, and fear came pouring out of his eyes, mingling with the mud and rain on Black Spot's neck.

A warm hand on his shoulder startled him, and he jerked away. His father towered over him, saying nothing. Then, slowly, he knelt down in the mud and wrapped his big arms around his son and the little pony, who stood patiently, allowing himself to be hugged by them both.

With tears still running down his face, Minko said, "Will you send Black Spot away again, Father?"

"No, my son. Your mother and I have made a decision. I will talk to the removal agent about it tomorrow. I am going to travel to Indian Territory on my own. I need to go ahead of the people and make a place for our family to come to. You will go with me, and now Black Spot will come too. You will keep your pony, because you have already given up more than enough to please the whites." Swinging his son up into his arms, Itilakna said, "Now come. We must sleep awhile before we go."

"But I have nothing with which to tie up Black Spot," Minko Ushi said.

Itilakna laughed quietly. "He has followed you all this way, and very cleverly too. He is not going anywhere without you."

PART
II
October 26–November 17, 1831

Chapter Four

Minko Ushi slept soundly and woke to a cold rain that was quickly turning to sleet. When he rushed outside to look for Black Spot, the sky was so dark it looked like night. As he walked through the camp, he saw that some of the people had no shelter but had spent the night wrapped in their blankets, trying to sleep under the big oak trees. Even though there would be no sun this day, they had spread the soggy blankets on the bushes to dry them. Smoky campfires struggled to burn wet wood, and whole families crowded onto tiny patches of high ground. The people had not been prepared for this kind of weather, and small children ran among the tents, some wearing thin dresses or shirts, others nothing at all. The noises of early morning were mixed with the sounds of coughing and crying and angry voices.

Minko Ushi stood in the midst of all this misery and was

suddenly so angry that he wanted to shout and throw stones at whoever had caused it. He had to find Black Spot. They would be leaving soon, and he would be glad to go.

He was beginning to think Black Spot had run away when he saw the black-eyed face peeking from behind a tree. It disappeared, and Minko ran to catch the pony, but when he got to the tree, Black Spot was nowhere to be found.

Bushes rattled off to the left, and again Minko Ushi rushed toward the sound. The little pony was hiding behind a small tree, but only his head was hidden. The rest of him was sticking out as plain as could be. This time, Minko Ushi quietly circled around the tree and surprised Black Spot from behind. "So, you want to play, do you?" Minko Ushi laughed delightedly at the pony's almost human look of surprise. Just then, Itilakna's familiar whistle sounded across the camp.

"Come on, Black Spot! We are going to Indian Territory!"

Minko Ushi found his father on the far edge of the camp. Itilakna told him, "The agent says that if we go on our own, we will be given ten dollars in gold, a new rifle, and food and supplies for the trail."

"And Black Spot will be allowed to come with us?" Minko asked.

"He is yours and he will come with us. As with all things the white man does, walking requires that papers be filled out. This will take some days, but we will not wait. We can have the rifle today, and the gold will be given to your mother at the military post called Fort Smith. We will leave soon after midday. Now, go say your good-byes."

Taking leave of his mother was not easy. Her black eyes

were shiny with unshed tears, but she finished braiding her hair and then held her arms out to him. She pulled him close and tried to hide her fear, but he smelled it, the way he could smell snakes when they were near. He did his best to calm her.

"This is a great adventure, Mother, but I know it will be dangerous, and I will be most careful. There is no need to worry."

She squeezed him so tightly he couldn't breathe. "Then I will not worry, my little warrior." He knew that this was not quite true, that she was just trying to be brave, so he put on his bravest face too and escaped as quickly as he could. He did not want to see her tears or let her see that his face was also wet. He looked back once and wished he had not. She stood by the wagon in her muddy dress with her hand pressed to her mouth, and he knew her tears mingled with the rain on her beautiful face.

They took only a little of the dried meat and corn, which went into a deerhide pouch along with Itilakna's prized bearskin, a small cooking pot, flint rock, leather stripping, and a small bundle of twigs and dry grass to kindle their campfire. They set off, with Black Spot following, to find a place to cross the Mississippi.

A long walk to the north brought them to a low place in the river. The water at the crossing place was chest-deep and swift, so Minko Ushi sat on his father's shoulders and held the rifle in his arms.

"Come, Black Spot!" he urged. But Black Spot waited until his people were halfway across the river before he jumped into the water.

Minko Ushi knew that horses were good swimmers, but

the current was swift, and the pony was so small that he had to struggle to keep from being carried away.

When father and son reached shallow water and Minko Ushi looked back, there was no sign of the loyal little pony.

"Don't worry, Son. Black Spot probably just got carried farther downstream. He'll be along soon." But Minko Ushi did worry. He kept looking back, hoping to see the familiar black-eyed face.

The late autumn sun dipped low in the western sky and darkness came quickly. They found shelter in a long-abandoned log cabin, which was missing most of its roof and one of its walls. Even though the icy rains continued, Itilakna managed a small campfire. They ate some of the meat and corn, and tried to dry out as best they could.

"Father, do you think we should go looking for Black Spot?"

"No, Minko Ushi. I think we should get some sleep. We must get an early start because we have many days and nights to travel. It will be a hard journey. All I know of the way is that we must follow the old trails and the setting sun."

"You mean that you don't know the way to go?" Minko Ushi was astonished, for he believed his father knew everything.

Itilakna chuckled. "Some of the young men who decided to walk went with a guide provided by the government. They all got lost somewhere on the other side of the Arkansas River and wandered around for several weeks. A scouting party finally found them. The government guide got lost when he tried to go find someone to give him directions. They never did find him."

"They got lost? But Father, Chata never get lost! Even I know that you travel in a straight line until you see markers to direct you. Were there no broken branches pointing the way?"

"This is a new trail for us, Son. Very few Chata have traveled this way. There were no markers for them to follow. They were relying on the guide. So even if there are markers, they may have been left by those young men and their government guide. I have seen nothing yet, but if I do, I will pay no attention."

Itilakna was still chuckling to himself as he settled in for the night. Minko Ushi was tired and sleepy, but still he could not stop thinking about the lost young men, and about Black Spot. The world was getting stranger every day, and it was an uncomfortable feeling to lose things always taken for granted. He fell asleep calling to Black Spot in his dreams.

They awoke to find a light snow falling and a much colder day. Minko Ushi had never seen snow and was thrilled at the sight. He ran, arms outstretched, mouth open, trying to catch the flakes on his tongue, until his father was ready to go. Itilakna broke camp hurriedly as Minko Ushi looked around for his pony without success. He knew better than to try and delay his father, for his manner was urgent as he said, "This snow that is coming will be very heavy. We need to move as quickly as we can."

They started walking at a brisk pace, and soon after midday they came upon a scene that made them both laugh. Standing in a little clearing, calmly eating the last of the summer grass, stood Black Spot. He was plastered with mud and covered with dead leaves and twigs. Minko Ushi called to him and Black Spot looked up, grinned at them, and went back to eating his midday meal. Itilakna shook his head in amazement, and Minko Ushi called, "Come on, you silly old horse. We have far to go, and colder weather is coming."

Black Spot shook his head, sending mud and twigs flying from his mane. Then he put his nose down again to nibble the grass.

Minko Ushi went to the little pony and began to pull the remaining twigs and leaves from the muddy mane. "I am happy to see that you are well, Black Spot, but we must hurry now. You can eat when we stop for the night." He tugged gently on the pony's mane, but Black Spot ignored him and began to wander away, eating as he went.

"Come, Son. We are losing the light," Itilakna said, walking forward once more.

Minko stood for a moment between his father and Black Spot, and then hurried after Itilakna.

"We can go on, Father. Black Spot will be along in a while," Minko Ushi said. Itilakna smiled at his son's serious tone, and they walked on. Black Spot caught up with them at sunset.

Chapter Five

*T*hey made good time, covering about fifteen miles each day. At night they camped under the trees. The snow had begun to fall faster and the wind howled like a wolf. Food was getting harder to find, and father and son kept a sharp eye out for animal tracks. Black Spot had been staying close to his people, and Minko Ushi was glad to have one less worry.

One day they spotted a deer. Itilakna was stringing his bow when Minko Ushi said quietly, "Look, Father. She has a little one with her."

Sure enough, the little fawn came running to her mother on delicate legs. Still so young that she had white spots on her back, the fawn was clumsily trying to coax her mother into a game of chase. Itilakna put his bow away, and they watched the deer for a few minutes before going on.

Minko Ushi was pleased that his father had not killed the

deer, but he wondered why he had not. He thought about it awhile and then asked, "Why didn't you kill the deer, Father?"

"If we had killed the mother, the little one would have suffered and died in time. I could not kill the little one, because if it died before its time, the deer tribe would weaken and die out."

Minko Ushi understood this, for his people believed that the children were the promise of the tribe's future. It seemed right that the same should be true for the animal tribes.

They traveled quickly. Each night they would stop and cook whatever they had been able to find. Late on the seventh day of their journey, the snow began to fall so hard that they could not see more than a little way ahead of them.

Minko Ushi's delight in the snow had faded. As it piled up on the trail and froze his feet, he began to dread the walk ahead. His father gave him the bearskin to wrap himself in and tied strips of it, fur side in, around Minko Ushi's feet. The leather strips made walking hard. The fur was heavy, and the strips were slippery against the snow, which was well past his ankles in some places.

Though Minko Ushi never complained, when the going got really hard, his father insisted that Minko ride on Black Spot's back. The little pony was agreeable enough, and they made better progress, but soon it was obvious that they could go no farther with the snow piling up so quickly. Early on the eighth day, soon after crossing the White River, they were forced to stop and build a shelter. They were still five or six days' walk from Little Rock, in Arkansas Territory.

Itilakna chose a spot under a stand of blackjack trees. He cut willow branches and tied them together with thin strips of leather to make a two-person shelter. Together, father and son gathered evergreen branches and tied them to the little mound-shaped shelter. More evergreen branches went inside, once the snow was cleared away.

Glad to be out of the blinding snow and the wind that cut through them like a knife, they rested in the little shelter. The wind and snow blew so hard that it wasn't possible to build a fire. All they could do was wait for the storm to ease up.

They ate the last little bit of jerky and corn, and went to sleep. It snowed for the rest of that day and through the night. The next morning, a thick layer of snow had sealed the little hut, and it was almost warm inside. They dug their way out of the shelter to find the snow still falling, but gently now, and the wind had stopped blowing so hard. The worst of the blizzard seemed to be over.

"We may be here for several days, Son. We need to rest and regain our strength."

They hurried about building a shelter for the fire. As Minko Ushi gathered saplings and helped cut down small trees to serve as lodge poles, he wondered where Black Spot had gone to spend the night.

They soon had a sturdy lean-to built into the side of an outcropping of rock, just a little way from the shelter. Now they needed to find dry wood to get a fire started, so they headed off into the woods. The ancient forest was so dense that the snow was just a couple of inches deep, and they were able to find a lot of fallen branches. Minko Ushi noticed a dark spot in the midst of all the white. Even though he was cold and wet and hungry, he could not resist the lure of the dark place. What he found was an opening in the rock, partly covered with brush and snow.

"Father, come and look. I think it is a cave." He started to pull away the brush, excited to have found a secret place, when he was jerked off his feet and carried away.

"Let us hope you did not wake the bears who live there," Itilakna said quietly to the wiggling boy under his arm.

"Bears? I saw no sign of bears," Minko said when he was set back on his feet.

"Let's get these branches back to camp, Son," Itilakna said.

"But, Father, why do you think there are bears there?"

"It was a warm, comfortable little cave. You have seen the claw marks on the trees. We are in some bear's territory. The chances are very good that the cave is a winter sleeping place.

"Sometimes you must trust your senses, your feelings, even if there is nothing to see or hear. Do you understand what I say, Minko?"

"I think I do. It is like fishing. I cannot see the fish, or hear them, but I know that they are there."

"Exactly so."

When they got back to camp, they found Black Spot standing under the lean-to, looking none the worse for his night in a blizzard.

"I was worried about you, my friend," Minko said to the pony. "I'll have a fire going in just a little while and we can get warm."

Itilakna patted the pony on the head. "I wonder if you are still so happy to be making this journey, little horse." Black Spot allowed himself to be patted and then stuck his head down to see what Minko Ushi was doing.

"I'm trying to break up these branches, Black Spot, and I don't have time to play," Minko said.

"You get the fire going, Minko Ushi, and I'll go see what I can find for us to eat," Itilakna said.

"I will, Father. Good luck."

With flint rock and twigs, Minko struggled to get the fire going. After many tries, the kindling finally began to burn. Slowly and carefully, Minko added the dead wood, and soon he had a blaze going.

"I think we must go for more wood, Black Spot. This fire was too hard to start, and we have to keep it burning."

They made two trips, getting the wood closest to camp and warming themselves by the fire after each trip. Black Spot was used to pulling wood tied to his halter and didn't seem to mind the work, and he made Minko's job much easier.

As Minko Ushi worked, he talked to Black Spot. "If Father sees what a good job I have done gathering wood, maybe he will let me go with him to hunt tomorrow. It is time I learned the proper way to hunt, you know." Black Spot had no opinion.

By the time Itilakna returned, just before sunset, Minko Ushi had a good pile of wood broken up.

"I got two rabbits, Son, and I see you have a nice fire going. We'll eat soon," Itilakna said as he began preparing the rabbits for cooking.

The moon was full and bright, and it looked as if the worst of the storm might be over, but the air was colder than it had been the day before.

As they ate their meal, Minko Ushi decided this would be a good time to ask his question.

"Father, do you think I could go with you to hunt tomorrow?"

Itilakna thought for a moment, then shook his head. "I know you want to help. But the snow is deep and the game so hard to find that I will have to move too quickly for you to keep up." He smiled at his son in the flickering light of the fire. "You will have to be head of the camp. It is an important job, for you must see that we have plenty of wood, and you must guard against intruders, both human and animal. Can you do this?"

"I can do it, Father. Black Spot will be my lookout. He has very good eyes and ears."

"It is settled then. Now we must sleep, so that I can get an early start in the morning."

They crawled into the hut, wiggling around to get comfortable in the small space. Minko Ushi fell asleep and dreamed of a green land with softly rolling hills and sky-blue water.

Itilakna left just after dawn. Minko Ushi slept for a while longer before going out to find Black Spot sleeping in the lean-to.

"Come on, you lazy horse. We have much to do today. I know it is very cold, but we can get the fire started and warm up before we go to gather wood."

They had already taken all the wood close to camp, so Minko Ushi and the pony had to go farther into the silent forest to find more. By midmorning he had gathered a good pile of branches. Some of them were large and heavy, and Minko was not sure how he was going to get them back to camp. Black Spot could not pull them because the leather cord might break.

Minko sat down on a fallen tree to think about it. Black Spot was busy pushing something around in the snow with his nose.

"What have you found, my friend?" Minko asked as he went to see.

Peeking through the snow were black walnuts, still wrapped in their bright green covers.

"Good work, Black Spot! There are enough of these to make a good meal. If only there were berries." Minko began looking around, searching for blackberry bushes. He was sure there must be some in this forest, which was so much like the woods at home.

In a few minutes he had found some thorny blackberry bushes. "Come on, Black Spot," he said excitedly. "We may be able to add something to the meat that Father brings back." The sudden winter storm had frozen the ripe fruit on the vine, and a little digging under the snow revealed a good amount of the frozen berries. Minko couldn't resist eating some of the fruit, and even Black Spot had a few, though he didn't seem to care for them much.

Using his cloth shirt as a basket, he carried the berries back to camp, and Black Spot pulled some of the smaller branches. It was slow going to keep the berries from spilling and, at the same time, to keep the branches from getting tangled up with Black Spot's legs.

It was getting late, but Father had not returned. There was still time to gather the walnuts and collect some more wood.

"Come on, Black Spot. We must hurry if we are to surprise Father."

Itilakna returned just at sunset. He came slowly and empty-handed, and he looked as if he were nearly frozen. As Itilakna sat down near the fire, Minko smiled to see the look of surprise on his father's face.

"Do I smell berry soup?" he asked as he peered into the little cookpot.

"Are you surprised, Father?" Minko asked, grinning delightedly.

"You are always surprising me, my son."

"Good! Let's eat. I'm so hungry, I could hardly wait for you," Minko said as he dipped the thick, sweet soup into gourd bowls.

"Where did you find nuts and berries in this snow? And where did you learn to make this soup?" Itilakna asked as he began eating.

"Black Spot found the nuts, and I found the berries. We are a good team, don't you think?"

"You are a very good team, and I am lucky to have you both with me. And where did you learn to make this soup?"

"From Mother," Minko said shyly. "She said there was no reason that I should not learn to cook. I did not want to at first, but you know how Mother is."

"Yes, I know how she is. She made me learn too," Itilakna said, grinning at his son. "But you must never tell anyone," he said hurriedly. "If my friends find out, I will have to cook every time we go on a hunt."

"You say nothing about me, and I will not tell on you," Minko Ushi said, his eyes sparkling in the firelight.

"Even now, your mother reaches out to care for us," Itilakna said quietly.

They sat in silence for a while in the vast frozen world that surrounded them, and when the fire burned low, they slept.

Chapter Six

*I*tilakna left before Minko Ushi awoke the next morning. The snow was falling again, and Minko hurried to rekindle the fire. The morning was still and the silence in the white world was a little unsettling. In the woods at home, there was always the sound of birds or animals calling to one another, but in this alien whiteness, all was silent.

Suddenly feeling very alone, Minko Ushi looked around for Black Spot. Then he noticed the tracks running along beside his father's. Black Spot had decided to follow Itilakna on the hunt.

Minko Ushi threw up his hands and shouted, "You foolish old horse! You know we have work to do. Why do you go off like this? Why, I ask you?"

The sound of his own voice broke the spell of silence, and

he stomped around until his anger was spent. Then he prepared to go into the woods to see if there were more berries and nuts and to bring more of the branches he had found yesterday.

He emptied the supply pouch and put everything in the shelter. He would need something to carry the nuts and berries he hoped to find. He started out, practicing whistling to chase away the silence.

It was midmorning by the time he had gathered all the remaining nuts and berries. Once that was done, he began pulling branches from yesterday's pile, all the time wondering how he would get them to camp.

He sat down to rest and realized that he was very tired and very hungry. The cold seemed to creep beneath his clothes, settling against his skin and making his teeth chatter. He ate a few berries and felt a little better.

Then Minko tied the pouch around his neck and struggled to get one of the long tree branches under his arm and one in each hand. He went only a little way before he had to rest again. He knew this was not going to work, so he abandoned one of the branches and made his way slowly back to camp.

Itilakna met Minko Ushi as the boy was coming out of the woods.

"Let me help you, Son," Itilakna said, taking the branches.

"Thank you, Father. I seem to be moving too slowly today," Minko said, glad to hand over his burden.

"You just need food, and I am pleased to say that we will have a fat beaver in our cooking pot this day."

"I am happy to hear that. Berries and nuts are good, but they do not stop my stomach from growling at me."

"Why don't you sleep for a while, and when you wake up, we will eat."

"But I have to bring in the rest of the wood and it will be dark soon. I would have finished my work, but Black Spot followed you and I had no help," Minko Ushi said, trying to recall his anger, but failing. All he felt was his tiredness.

"You sleep, Son, and I'll take care of everything. You have done a good job, and now you must rest. Go now." Minko Ushi went gladly.

When he woke, it was dark. The wonderful smell of cooking meat reached his nose and pulled him from the shelter. Black Spot had returned and joined them near the fire as they were eating.

"Now is a fine time for you to return, after all the work is done," Minko Ushi said to the little pony. Black Spot looked at his friend, grinned his big horsey grin, and nibbled at Minko's hair.

This struck Itilakna as very funny. He started laughing, and Black Spot joined him, throwing back his head and hee-hawing like a donkey. Minko Ushi shook his head in disgust, but the laughter came bubbling up. Then they were all laughing, and it was a good feeling.

The next morning, Itilakna woke his son by calling that it was time to eat. Minko felt good and was ready to do whatever needed doing. When they finished eating the last of the beaver, Itilakna prepared to go out hunting.

"We have plenty of wood, Son, so you should stay close to camp today. If you want something to do, you can make a wind screen for the lean-to. I hope to be back before too long."

"I wish you good hunting, Father. I will be happy to stay here and guard the camp today."

Minko collected willow branches and began to strip them down. By early afternoon he decided to take a break and see what Black Spot was up to.

There had been nothing to feed the pony, and though he had grown a little leaner, he seemed to be finding enough food to keep him going. Minko Ushi watched him now and saw him pushing the snow away with his nose, nibbling at the dead leaves and frozen grass beneath. He also nibbled at the bark on the trees and the tips of the branches he could reach. To help him, Minko climbed a tree and held down the branches.

When he had eaten his fill, Black Spot lay down in the snow and wiggled around on his back, kicking his hooves in the air. It looked like so much fun Minko decided to join him. They wiggled and kicked and pushed snow onto each other, and Minko laughed so hard it made his sides hurt. That's where Itilakna found them, and he was pleased to see his son playing and laughing. He waved the two big catfish he had caught and shouted that hot food would be ready soon. The wind screen was never built.

The next day the weather cleared a little, though it was still bitterly cold. Itilakna's hunt was good, and he took a small buck. The following morning he felt they should move on before the weather turned bad again. They loaded the supplies in the pouch, along with the rest of the deer meat, and began walking west once more.

"We have been delayed by seven days, but at least we are alive," Itilakna observed. "And I have made another decision, Minko. We will be going to Fort Smith after we leave Little Rock. We will go there to get the supplies the government promised us and use them to build a cabin in Indian Territory and plant crops in the spring. I had hoped never to deal with the government again, but I think I am going to need all the help I can get."

Minko Ushi was riding Black Spot. He hated being so helpless, but the snow was just too deep for him to keep up. "When we get to Indian Territory, Father, I want to help build the cabin," he said.

"I have come to depend on your help, Son, so we will build the cabin together."

"And you know, Father, I am looking forward to seeing a village where the white people live. Do they live as we do?"

"I think they live much the same as we do, but they are very different in the things they believe."

"In what way?" Minko asked, shifting around to get comfortable.

"For one thing, they seem to think they can own the land. They believe that if they have a paper with words on it, the earth they live on is theirs." Itilakna was smiling broadly.

Minko Ushi shook his head, as he had seen the elders do. "Do you think they will ever return to the land of their ancestors?"

Itilakna stopped smiling and shook his head. "No, Son, they are here to stay. We must learn to live with them, or they will kill us. Not just the Chata, but all Indians everywhere," he said, using the English word *Indians*.

They walked on in silence, and soon all else was forgotten as they struggled to cover the distance ahead of them, following the snow-covered trails. When they came to a stand of cane that stretched farther than Minko could see, Itilakna spent the rest of the day hacking a way through it. They slept that night huddled beneath the low-hanging branches of a giant pine tree.

They spent the next three days trying to get around overflowing creeks and dangerous swamp ground that was frozen on the surface but cracked beneath their feet when they tried to pass. They walked for half a day out of their way and spent another half a day getting back on the trail. Each night they built a fire and cooked a little of the deer meat, but only a little. They had not seen one living thing in the frozen wilderness. Even the rabbits seemed to be in hiding. Father and son did not talk much during those four days; it was just too great an effort.

They were exhausted and so cold that their faces felt frozen. The snow was falling again, softly and silently. Minko sat on his little pony, his head bowed, chin on his chest as Itilakna led them along. It was the evening of the fourth day after leaving the shelter, and they were still at least two days' walk from Little Rock, maybe longer, if they ran into any more trouble.

"We will go just a little farther and find a place to sleep,"

Itilakna said. Minko Ushi knew that his father was feeling bad about bringing him on this cold and dangerous journey. Minko was about to speak when he heard his father grunt. Black Spot jerked forward, moving quickly. When he looked up, all Minko Ushi could see was his father's back, and then he saw the reason for the grunt. It was a cabin! Sitting out here in the middle of this deadly white world, it was the most wonderful thing Minko had ever seen. He was so relieved, he could have cried. It crossed his mind that he had felt like crying far too often lately, but he was too cold and tired to think about it.

As they neared the cabin, another thought froze his heart. What if the people who lived here were like Wagon Master Timmons? People who hated Indians. Was Wagon Master Timmons the only white person who hated them, or were there more? Fear was beginning to take hold, chasing away the desire to be in a warm place, when he heard Itilakna speaking again. "No tracks. No smoke from the chimney. This place is empty."

Minko Ushi tried to smile, and it felt as if his face were cracking.

There was a little barn for Black Spot, and as cold as he was, Minko insisted on taking his pony inside. They found a feed bin with a few oats and clean, dry hay to sleep on. Once Black Spot started eating, he had no time for Minko Ushi, so Minko patted the horse on the head and hurried into the house.

Itilakna had found wood in a bin outside the back door and had a fire roaring in the fireplace. He melted snow in an old cooking pot and threw in the deer meat. When Minko found a sack of corn, forgotten by the people who had moved away, he threw several handfuls of that into the pot too. While they waited for the corn soup to cook, they explored the little farmhouse.

The main feature of the cabin was the big fireplace. It took up nearly half of the west wall and was big enough for a small child to walk into. The cabin was built of whole logs, and the spaces between were filled with a mixture of mud and straw, which had dried as hard as brick. It had only two rooms. This one large room served as living space and kitchen, and a second, much smaller room was for sleeping. It was clear that the house had not stood empty for very long, for it was clean and tidy, as if the mistress had just stepped out for a moment. All that remained of the furnishings was a broken butter churn, sitting in one corner, and a rickety old wooden chair.

"Why do you think the people left, Father?" Minko asked as he looked around the snug little cabin.

"Farming is a hard life. You are at the mercy of the sun and rain and cold. It may be that these people were not prepared to suffer such hardships." Itilakna pointed to the sack of corn. "Maybe that is all they had to show for a year's work, so they moved on, looking for an easier life."

"I remember when our corn and squash did not do well, but we did not leave our home," Minko said.

"That is because we live in a village where we all help one another. The whites who come out here live as these people did, all alone. It is no wonder that they cannot survive."

They sat silently for a moment, and then Itilakna said, "Come, let us see if we may eat yet." The corn soup tasted even better than it smelled, and between mouthfuls, Minko spoke of the things on his mind. "What is this place of the little rock?"

"Little Rock is a village on the river, and if luck is with us, there will be a boat to take us upriver to Fort Smith," Itilakna said, refilling their bowls with soup.

"Why do you think there will be a boat at the place of Little Rock?" Minko asked, blowing on his hot soup.

"The agent at Memphis said it would be so, but I put very little faith in that," Itilakna said, grinning at his son over the gourd bowl.

"Will Mother be there, do you think?" Minko asked quietly.

"It may be, for that is where they will take our people when they leave Memphis. Perhaps we will see her there," Itilakna said, but he did not sound at all hopeful.

They ate their fill of the wonderful soup and then fixed themselves a place to sleep in front of the fire. It felt so good to be warm and full, and not have to sleep rolled up in a ball, that Minko Ushi was drifting into sleep almost as soon as he lay down. Thoughts of his mother and grandparents made him look at his father, who sat staring into the fire.

"Are they well, Father? Mother and my grandparents, I mean."

Itilakna looked at his son for a moment, and Minko guessed that his father had been thinking the same thing.

"We have to believe they are well," he finally said. "Your

mother is one of the strongest people I know. Does she not get me to do everything she wants, without raising her voice? And does she not take care of all of us, no matter what we may ask of her? She is well. They are all well."

"I am sure you are right, Father. It is just that I worry sometimes."

Itilakna looked at the boy, who was so like his mother, and smiled. "I worry too, sometimes."

In that mysterious land between sleep and waking, Minko dreamed. His mother stood before a cabin that looked much like their old home, holding out her arms to him. He ran to her, and wrapped in that warm embrace, he felt safe and happy for the first time in many weeks.

Chapter Seven

*T*hey stayed in the farmhouse for two more days. Itilakna went out hunting both days, but all he could find were two rabbits each day. These four rabbits they saved to take with them. Minko did not want to leave the warm little cabin, but he said nothing to his father. The snow had nearly stopped, and it was time to move on.

Minko Ushi went out to the barn and tried to slip the halter over Black Spot's head, but the little pony would have none of it. He jerked his head up and down and backed away.

"What is wrong with you, Black Spot? You know we cannot stay here. Now come, you are wasting time." The pony paid no attention to Minko but went back to nibbling on the hay. Minko walked toward him, talking softly. "Come on, my good friend, we must go now." When he got close enough to throw the halter on, Black Spot trotted toward the barn door and turned around to look at his friend.

"I do not have time for this, Black Spot. I will send Father out here, and he will put this on you."

Black Spot took a few steps sideways as Minko started toward him once again.

"Very well, then. I will send Father," Minko said angrily and went to find his father.

Itilakna listened to his son's story and did his best not to smile. "You know that Black Spot has a mind of his own. I think he knows what he must do, but he does not always like it.

"He is rather like the Chata people, don't you think? He has been through a great deal, but still he is full of life and spirit, and he challenges us, defies us to break him."

"That may be so, Father, but he still is the most stubborn creature I have ever seen," Minko said indignantly.

"Well, I will see what I can do," Itilakna said.

Black Spot watched the man come into the barn and then started backing up until he was stopped by the wall. He rolled his eyes and shook his head, looking as if he were going to rear up on his hind legs. He never got the chance. Itilakna was as quick as a striking rattler, and the halter was on before the little pony even realized what was happening. Black Spot stood there quietly, and they looked at one another, man and horse.

"Come on, horse. It is time to go," Itilakna said. He turned and walked away with the lead in his hand. Black Spot waited until the lead was stretched tight, then jerked his head back. The sudden jerk spun Itilakna halfway around, and he nearly lost his footing. He looked at the pony in disbelief, and then he started to laugh.

"Minko is right," he said. "You are indeed a stubborn creature, but we must go. If you will come, we will take some of this nice hay for you to eat." Itilakna reached down, picked up some hay, and shook it. "What do you say?" He pulled on the lead, and the little horse came forward a bit and then stopped again. Itilakna pulled harder and Black Spot resisted. Itilakna pulled harder still, and Black Spot backed up, planted all four of his legs, and would not be moved.

"See what I told you, Father?" Minko Ushi said from the doorway of the barn. "He is impossible. We will have to leave him here."

Itilakna looked at the little pony for a moment and then dropped the lead. "Take the halter off of him, Minko, or he'll get tangled up in it." He looked straight at the horse and said, "Do you not care that Minko will have to walk through the snow unless you let him ride?" The horse continued to look at Itilakna for a moment and then calmly returned to nibbling on the hay.

Minko Ushi took the halter off and hugged the pony. "We will see you when you catch up with us, but don't be too long. I am no longer angry with you, so do not make me worry too much."

And so they walked away, and Black Spot stood in the doorway of the barn and jerked his head up and down as if waving good-bye.

They took the few supplies they had found at the farmhouse. The extra weight slowed them down so that they were barely able to cover half their usual distance before evening overtook them. They camped in a thick stand of cedar trees and built a small fire. Though it was still very cold, Minko Ushi was able to keep fairly warm under the bearskin on a bed of cedar branches.

"Father, is this how our new home will be? Will there always be snow and cold?"

"No, Son. The government just chose a bad time to send us away. They say it is much like home there, though it does get colder than we are used to. Go to sleep now. We leave at dawn."

The next morning, Minko hated to get up and start through the snow. But now Little Rock was just a day or so away. He wondered why Black Spot had not caught up, but he wasn't really worried. The little pony seemed to be a survivor too.

The snow reached past Minko's knees. By midday they were tired and so cold that they were forced to stop and build a fire. It was not easy finding wood that would burn, but after a search, they managed to gather enough to get a fire going. It took a long time for Minko Ushi to thaw out, and though they were wasting valuable time, it could not be helped. Itilakna cooked some of the corn and one of the rabbits and decided that they would spend the night and start out again tomorrow.

"We may have to travel for a shorter time each day," Itilakna said, stirring the fire. "The early morning still carries the cold of the night, so we will leave when the sun is higher in the sky and travel until dark. That may be a little easier on both of us." He looked at his son closely to see how he would accept this idea.

Minko Ushi spooned the soup into his mouth and took some time to answer.

"It is true that I do not like to get up so early and start walking. And it is also true that it is very cold at dawn, but I want to walk as far as we can each day, because this part of the journey is almost over." He looked at his father and smiled a faint little smile. "And to tell you the truth, I am ready for it to be over."

"I am ready for that too, Son," Itilakna said. "We will leave when the sun is well up and go as far as we can. If we must stop and rest, then we will."

They woke the next morning to clear skies and a weak sun that gave no warmth. Nevertheless, Minko Ushi was glad to feel the sun on his face again. Black Spot was still missing, so Minko rode on his father's shoulders for a while and then walked until he started to fall behind again. They made better time this way, but Minko Ushi knew that it was hard on his father, and he did his very best to keep up. Sometimes the trail was hard to see because of all the snow, but Itilakna rarely hesitated before deciding which way to go. They were walking along a rocky trail that would take them across a hill and down into a snowy valley.

They stopped at the top of the hill for a short rest. As they looked out over the valley, Minko saw smoke off in the distance. Itilakna saw it too.

He pointed and said, "Little Rock. If we make good time, we will be there in one more day."

Minko was so cheered by the sight that he did a few steps of the eagle dance. "Eeee-Yah! Eeee-Yah!" he shouted into the air.

Itilakna laughed out loud at this unexpected display of energy. "You are more like your little pony than you know," he said. "Full of surprises."

They made camp early, a few miles into the valley, and cooked another of the rabbits. As the sun set, it grew even colder under the clear, starry skies, and father and son slept huddled together, trying to stay warm.

Minko Ushi woke early and lay watching the stars fade from the sky. The world was so silent and still, it was easy to think that he and his father were the only ones living on the earth. It was a very scary feeling. They had seen no one since they left Memphis. What if this winter storm had killed everyone?

Of course, they had seen the smoke from the houses in Little Rock, so there must be people there. He was suddenly very anxious to get to the village of Little Rock. He needed to know that he and his father were not alone in the world. He fell asleep again and was awakened by his father getting up to stir the fire. The sky was just growing light in the east.

"Do you think we should leave now, Father? We could stop to eat farther down the trail."

"No, Son. We need to eat now, and we will not stop again until we are in Little Rock. We will need to move quickly to get there before dark, but I believe we can do it."

"What can I do to help?" Minko asked, crawling out from the warmth of the bearskin.

"If you will throw some wood on the fire, I will see to the food," Itilakna said.

They walked into Little Rock just at sunset. Minko looked around in wonder at the many wooden buildings lining both sides of the deeply rutted, muddy roads. Instead of being in their warm homes, people were on the wooden walkways and driving wagons along the slushy streets. Itilakna spotted a black man coming out of one of the buildings and, pulling

Minko along, hurried to ask him where he might find the Indian Agent. He began speaking slowly in English, trying to make himself understood, when the man said in recognizable Choctaw, "How can I help you, friend?"

"I am looking for the Indian Agent," Itilakna said, smiling.

"He's over in the place with the red door," he said, pointing across the street to a small, shabby building.

Itilakna nodded his head in thanks and started to walk away.

"Say, friend," the black man said in English. "When you git done with that bloodsucker, y'all come on down to the livery stable. Supper'll be ready, and I'd be proud if you'd eat with me."

"You are very kind, and my son and I may well accept your offer," Itilakna said.

"Good. Good," said the man. "Go down to the end of the street, and I'm just off to your left," he said, waving his hand toward the north end of town.

Itilakna nodded once again, and the man turned and walked away, pulling his coat closer around him.

They stood looking after the man for a moment and then headed for the building with the red door.

The removal agent was a tall, thin man who kept pushing his sliding spectacles back up on his nose. "I am sorry to say, sir, that your people have not yet arrived," he said. "The plan now is to move them all by wagon. They should be on the road somewhere between here and Arkansas Post. But the roads were badly damaged by this blasted storm, and it's put us at least two weeks behind schedule." The agent spoke the soft and musical Choctaw language in a funny, clipped sort of way, and Minko Ushi slapped his hand over his mouth to stop the giggles from coming out. He looked around the small room. It looked much like the log cabin they had stayed in so many miles back along the trail.

The men stood in front of the fireplace, talking. Minko, meanwhile, was drawn away to the big desk sitting near the south wall. It contained many stacks of papers, and maps, and an inkwell and quill pen. There was also a most fascinating thing in a small silver frame. Inside the frame was a tiny woman holding a small child. Minko stared at the thing for several minutes, trying to see if the woman or her child moved, but they remained as they were. How had the agent captured these tiny people, and why were they so still?

He reached for the silver frame, then jerked his hand back when the agent's voice boomed around the little room.

"Don't touch anything on that desk, boy."

Minko Ushi went to stand beside his father, watching the agent's face to see if there was to be any more shouting, but the agent was busy talking to Itilakna again.

"As I said, Mr. Itilakna, it will be at least two weeks before your people get here. You can find someplace to stay and wait for them, or I can let you have some supplies and you can continue on your own."

"Is there a boat to take us upriver to Fort Smith?" Itilakna asked.

The agent shook his head, and his glasses slid down his nose. "The army took the two boats that were here to move some of their troops, so there is nothing available. I just hope," he said, pushing his glasses back up, "that they return the boats before your people get here."

Itilakna nodded his head as if this was exactly what he had expected. "We will take the supplies and see if we can find a way upriver."

"Very good. Let me write out a supply order for you, and you can pick them up at the supply house tomorrow." The agent hurried to his desk and began to shuffle his papers. "Here we go," he said, waving one of the papers. "Just let me fill this out and you can be on your way."

He scratched on the paper with the quill pen and then handed Itilakna the paper. "The supply house is right on the dock; you can find it easily. Good luck to you, Mr. Itilakna."

Minko Ushi and his father left the warm office and stepped out into the quickly gathering dusk. Itilakna tucked the paper into his pouch and looked around the village as if wondering what to do next. Minko decided to help him make up his mind.

"Will we go to eat with the black man?" he asked as his stomach rumbled at him.

Before Itilakna could answer, Minko spotted a familiar white shape bouncing along the muddy street.

"Father, look! It's Black Spot."

The pony trotted up to his friend and stood, looking expectantly at him.

"I think your horse is hungry too," Itilakna said, "so we will be calling on the man from the livery stable."

"Come on in out of the cold," the man said in Choctaw as he opened the door for them. "Nice little pony you got there, son. Could he do with some oats?"

Minko nodded yes, smiling shyly at the friendly man.

"Well, bring him on in," he said, opening the door wider for Black Spot.

They entered through a door on the east side of the livery, into a small room set up as living quarters. There was an army cot with a pile of blankets on it, a large woodstove for heating and cooking, and a small wooden table and one chair. Another door was on the other side of the room. Minko and the man went through this door into the livery stable, followed by Black Spot. The pony switched his tail and lifted his head as though he were taking in all the good smells.

"There's a bag of oats over in that corner," the man said, switching to English. "You tend to your friend, then come on back 'cause we're fixin' to eat."

"I will be quick," said Minko, and he was, because the smells from the stove were hurrying him along. It felt good to be warm again.

Chapter Eight

Minko came back in the room as the men were shaking hands.

"My name's John Turner, and I'm pleased to meet you," the man was saying. "Guess I got so cold I forgot my manners a while ago. Y'all can call me John."

"I am Itilakna, and my son is Minko Ushi. We are grateful for your offer of food."

"Well, let's git to eatin' then," John Turner said. "Come on, son, and help me pull up these here chairs. It's been a long time since I had company to supper, and I'll be blessed if I can recollect the last time I used them." Minko helped him pull two dusty chairs out of a corner and over to the sturdy homemade table.

"Y'all sit down, and I'll git this food served up," John said as he began dipping food out of the bubbling pots. Minko was fascinated by the shiny black stove. He had never seen anything like it. It looked like a big storage chest, but it was made of metal, with a big door in front. He watched as John opened this door and took out a pan of cornbread, using a piece of cloth so his hand wouldn't get burned. He set the bread on the table and then used a big spoon to dip beans from a pot into a bowl. From another pot he took mustard greens, and from a covered iron skillet came fried chicken.

Try as he might, Minko could not see the fire. He could hear it and feel it, but it was invisible. Was this black box magic? It must be if it could cook all of this food at the same time with invisible fire.

The food was good, and Minko ate until he thought he might explode. Every once in a while, he looked at the mysterious black stove.

"What's troublin' you 'bout that stove, Minko Ushi?" John asked as he sopped up the last of the bean soup with his cornbread.

Minko looked at John and smiled his shy smile. "Is the box magic? Where is the fire?"

John chuckled. "Well, maybe it is sorta magic, now that you mention it. I bought it from a city fella who came out here and brought all this fancy stuff with him. He couldn't stand all the wilderness, though. Packed up his clothes, auctioned off all his newfangled stuff, and went back east."

John got up and went over to the stove. "Come have a look," he said. He took a bent piece of metal and lifted one of the four round covers from the top of the stove. Itilakna and Minko looked inside and saw the bright red embers of burning wood.

"That's the firebox, and it heats up the top of the stove and the oven too. Darn thing even has a place to heat water, for washin' dishes or takin' a bath." He pointed to a metal tank attached to the side of the stove.

Itilakna smiled and shook his head, but Minko was enchanted with this new thing and continued his inspection while John and Itilakna sat down to drink coffee. Having traded some of his best corn for coffee last summer, Itilakna found he had a taste for this white man's brew. He sipped the hot coffee and smiled at John Turner. "How is it you speak my language?" he asked.

"Well, I'll tell ya," John said, settling back in his chair. "Your people gave my family refuge when they were tryin' to escape from a Mississippi cotton plantation. The language was sort of passed on from my grandparents. Wasn't for the Choctaws, I'd most likely been born a slave, 'stead of ownin' my own livery stable." He stirred a little more sugar into his coffee. "May as well tell ya what else I been thinkin' too. This is a bad, bad thing the government is doin' to your people. Ain't no way to fight 'em neither, and they know it. It's a death march, Itilakna, and I'm thinkin' that's just what they intended."

Minko Ushi came to stand beside his father, for there was very little that escaped his keen hearing, and he wanted to know how his father felt about John Turner's words.

Itilakna sat quietly, staring straight ahead. Minko began to think his father would not speak, but then he turned to John and said, "All that you say may be true, and if I think too much about it, the anger takes over and I cannot think clearly." He sighed deeply. "I have to think of my family. If I were alone, I

would fight them until they killed me, but I cannot. It is the same with most of the others. Our task now is to see that we survive as a people."

John Turner nodded in agreement. "Reckon you're right 'bout that, but it still makes me so mad, I could spit nails."

"You are a kind man, John Turner, and I am happy to know you," Itilakna said to his host.

John offered them shelter for the night in his barn. They retired early and slept well in the warm hay, which still smelled of the summer meadow. It brought back memories of home, and Minko Ushi felt a great sadness, but he did not cry. There was no use.

Just after sunrise, Black Spot began nibbling at Minko's hair. Minko pushed him away and settled deeper under the covers that John Turner had loaned them. A few minutes later, the persistent pony was dragging the blankets across the floor. Minko sat up, made a grab for them, and missed, and Black Spot trotted away, head held high.

"What is wrong with you, you crazy horse?" Minko demanded, going after his blankets.

The little pony dropped the covers and trotted over to the feed bin. He stood waiting there.

"Could you not wait until I got up on my own?" Minko grumbled, pouring oats into the feed bin.

John Turner had been watching from the doorway. "Who's in charge here, anyhow?" He laughed.

"I am sure Black Spot thinks he is in charge," Minko said, slapping the pony on the flank. Black Spot didn't even notice.

John laughed again and said, "You and your pa come on and eat, 'fore it gets cold."

They ate hot oatmeal and fresh-made biscuits. John Turner offered to take them to the dock to pick up their supplies and to see if they could arrange for a ride upriver to Fort Smith. He also packed biscuits and dried beef for them to take along.

"It's tough goin' west of the river, worse than what you already been through," he said as they walked to the dock. Itilakna nodded his head as if this too was exactly what he had expected.

Minko Ushi was facinated by the sights and sounds at the dock. The river was low, and John explained that travel had been limited to the deep water channel for some time. But the water level had risen some due to rain and snow up north. The dock workers and crews of the various small boats were busy loading and unloading supplies, fish, furniture, and many other things Minko could not identify. It smelled strongly of fish and river water here, and the men called loudly to one another in the confusing English language. No one paid any attention to them, and John Turner looked around until he spotted someone he knew.

"Y'all wait here, and I'll go talk to ol' Jacob and see if I can git you a ride, if he's goin' upriver," he said. Itilakna and Minko watched as their new friend walked down the dock and began talking to a short man with a fur hat. Minko wanted to see how things looked from the edge of the dock, so he left his father and went to peer over the side. It was not so very far down to the water, and he was amazed to see huge fish swimming just below the surface. He brushed away the snow and lay down on his stomach to get a better look. The fish were long and thin, and had long beaks filled with teeth that looked sharp and dangerous.

He heard John Turner's familiar chuckle. "Nasty lookin' things, ain't they, Minko?" Minko nodded, still staring at the ugly fish.

"They're called gars," John said. "Some folks'll eat 'em, but mostly they ain't good for nothin'. It's said they're as old as time itself, those fish, and I believe it. I've seen 'em get as big as alligators, and they sure 'nough look like monsters then. Too bad they ain't fit to eat."

"Come, Minko," Itilakna said. "John has found us a way upriver."

"Yep," John said. "I'll give Jacob two dollars, and he'll take y'all to Dwight Mission. That's 'bout halfway to Fort Smith. He says the pony can go for free. Now let's go pick up those supplies."

The government warehouse was being stocked with supplies from the boats, and the supervisor was clearly impatient with John's request to fill Itilakna's supply order. "You people stay right here, and I'll see if I can spare someone to fill this," he said. He hurried away through a maze of barrels and bales and hanging sides of beef.

"This stuff is s'posed to be for your people, but you'll never see it," John said disgustedly. "By this time tomorrow, the best of it will be gone to fill the larders of the agent and his cronies. Been goin' on for a lot o' months now, and it ain't likely to stop."

After they had waited a long time, a rough-looking man

handed John a burlap sack of supplies and walked away without saying a word. When they got outside, they looked to see what was in the sack. It turned out to be dried corn, dried beef, and something called hardtack, a saltless, rock-hard biscuit.

"Just as well throw that hardtack away," John said. "It's most likely years old and loaded with bugs." He dug it out of the sack, sniffed it, and broke it open. The inside had turned to powder and was filled with tiny black bugs. He gave all of it to Minko.

"Go feed it to the gars, son," he said, wiping the smelly stuff from his hands.

Minko caught up with them a few minutes later in front of a small, ugly boat. As they walked up the ramp, John Turner caught Minko's hand and slipped a five-dollar gold piece into it. He winked and put his finger to his lips.

Minko understood that he was to keep quiet about the gift and nodded.

Then John spoke to Itilakna. "I hope you can find someone at the mission who'll take you on to Fort Smith. I don't like to think of you and the boy out in this weather."

"We will be fine, John Turner. No need to worry about us," Itilakna said.

"I'll keep a watch for your wife and family, and do what I can to help."

Itilakna shook hands with the good-hearted man. "If ever you go to the Territory, you must come and visit with us, my friend. Maybe you could move your shop there. It would be good to have a friend in that place."

John Turner laughed and said, "Well, ya never know. I might just take a notion to do that very thing. Y'all have a safe trip, now."

Minko led his reluctant pony up the ramp. Black Spot went, but not happily, and the cold, lonely journey began again.

PART
III
November 18, 1831—June 21, 1832

Chapter Nine

*T*he captain of the little boat was a small, round man with more hair on his face, and sticking out from under his fur hat, than Minko had ever seen on any white man. As they got underway, Minko was certain he was not going to like this. The boat creaked and moaned and rolled from side to side, and Minko, with one arm around his jittery pony's neck and one hand gripping the railing, was starting to feel just as if he had eaten too many blackberries. He took deep breaths of the cold air and turned away from the water. That helped, but only a little.

Jacob Speers spoke in a friendly voice to Itilakna. "Whatcha doin' so far ahead of the other injuns, huh?" Itilakna understood the question but, not finding the words to answer, he said nothing. That didn't matter to Jacob. He kept right on talking. "Heard you people was givin' up a lot of land in Missasip' so's you can live in your own private territory. Must be real nice to have your own territory, huh? 'Bout time the government was givin' y'all somethin' back."

Itilakna stared at the round little man and shook his head in disbelief.

"Don't understand, huh? Well my advice to you is: Learn to speak American. If you plan to live in this here country, you oughta learn the lingo."

It was a full day's journey to Dwight Mission because of low water and the ever-spreading ice. When the sun set, the moonlight turned the world an icy, frozen blue. The strange black-and-blue-white landscape drifted by, the eerie silence broken only by the chug-chug of the boat's motor.

Minko Ushi stood at the rail for most of the journey. His stomach was still rolling, and he didn't want to embarrass himself by getting sick. Black Spot seemed to have adjusted to the rocking boat, but he stayed close to Minko, and every once in a while his skin rippled and shivered under Minko's hand. Itilakna stood beside his son and gazed out over the river, his face closed and unreadable.

Late that night they tied up at a tiny dock where a lantern glowed warmly in the night. They walked, the captain carrying the lantern, to a small rock church sitting in a grove of bare walnut trees.

The door was flung open before they knocked. They were greeted by a giant, clean-shaven man in a black suit that fit too tightly across his broad shoulders. Minko thought he was around the age of Itilakna, but with long, light-colored hair pulled into a ponytail and a big smile full of perfect teeth.

"Welcome, friend Jacob. I see you have brought us two

travelers. Welcome, friends!" He grabbed Itilakna's hand and pumped it up and down, smiling directly into Itilakna's eyes, something very few people were tall enough to do.

"Come in, come in please," he said. "Put your things here in the vestibule, and let's go into the kitchen. Hot food is waiting, and there's plenty for everyone."

"Folks, I'd like ya to meet the Reverend Luther Grant," Jacob said.

"We are pleased to be here, Reverend Grant," Itilakna said in slow English.

Black Spot started to follow his people into the church, but Minko Ushi stopped him. Reverend Grant's laughter boomed inside the empty church, and he said, "There's a stable in the back, son. Take the pony around and make him comfortable. Trudy will be glad of the company. She hasn't seen another horse in two weeks. Here, take this lantern with you."

The boy stared at this white giant who had spoken in flawless Choctaw. He had never heard a white man sound so much like a Choctaw. Itilakna gently pushed his son out the door, smiling at the boy's amazement.

The little pony trotted into the barn, and Minko closed the heavy door behind them. Trudy, the reverend's little bay, snorted and eyed them suspiciously. She was taller than Black Spot and had a shiny brown coat and big brown eyes.

The little pony walked up to Trudy and rubbed his nose against hers. She backed away but did not seem to mind the friendly gesture. Minko scooped oats out of a big burlap bag into the feeding trough, and both horses came over to eat. Satisfied that his horse would be happy with his new stable-mate, Minko returned to the church.

"Come and take your place, son. We're ready to eat," the Reverend Grant said in his booming voice. The four of them sat on benches at a long table, and the reverend and Jacob bowed their heads. "Our Heavenly Father, we ask that you bless the food we are about to receive, and bless too these travelers, who have come so far. Amen." The prayer was spoken in English, and Minko and his father sat quietly and watched the two men speak to their God.

"Amen," said Jacob. "Pass the taters, please." They ate boiled potatoes and fried cabbage and baked ham, with hot biscuits and strawberry preserves. Minko had become very fond of biscuits, and he loved the sweet preserves, made from wild strawberries. Whatever might be said of white people, he thought, they could cook some delicious food.

The Reverend Luther Grant told them that in addition to Choctaw, he spoke fluent Creek and Cherokee. "I was called by God," he explained, "to visit these tribes and convert them from their heathen ways and lead them to the rightful Creator." Speaking in Choctaw, and then switching to English for Jacob's benefit, he told them why the church was being closed.

"Since all the Indian Nations will eventually be moved to the Territory, we felt it would be good to relocate the mission there as quickly as possible. I am the last to leave. Jacob will take me to Little Rock to put some of my affairs in order, and then I will go to the new mission being built in the Territory. Perhaps I shall see you there, Itilakna?"

"You must know that our chief, Mushulatubbe, is much opposed to all missionaries and their teachings. He will never allow you to come to us to teach Christianity."

"Where is ol' Mushulatubbe?" the reverend asked, forking potatoes into his mouth.

"He is still trying to get the people ready to travel and may not go to Indian Territory until all of those from our district are on their way."

"Well, you are exactly right, Itilakna. Your chief wants nothing to do with anything Christian. That is precisely why we *must* be there, in case any of your people change their minds. It is our duty," said the Reverend Grant gleefully. Minko Ushi decided then and there that he would stop trying to understand the white man. It made his head hurt.

Minko Ushi and his father chose to spend the night in the empty chapel, and Jacob slept in the reverend's spare room. By the light of a flickering candle, Itilakna fixed them a place to sleep on the wooden floor. The church had been emptied of all its furnishings, except for the pulpit and a small crucifix on the wall behind it. Minko stood looking at the figure of a dying man nailed to a cross and wondered who he might be.

"Father, what is this place?" he asked, looking at the man on the cross once more. Itilakna peered into the shadows where his son stood and recognized one of the symbols of the Reverend Grant's God.

"This is where the Christians come to speak to their Great Father."

"And who is this sad-looking man on the cross?"

"I am not certain," Itilakna said.

"Was he a great warrior, then? And how did he come to be on this cross?"

"I believe he was a great speaker, but he was captured by

an enemy tribe and made to hang on that cross because they did not like the things he said."

Minko thought about this and then said, "He is the ancestor of some of the Christians but honored by them all, this I understand. But what has he to do with their Great Father?"

Itilakna considered for a moment and then said, "I cannot tell you that, Son, because I do not know. All I can say with any certainty is that they come to these places of worship every so often, and men like the Reverend Grant speak to them of the sacred writing." Itilakna blew out the candle and they lay down to sleep.

"I wonder why the whites must make even the simplest of things so confusing, Father."

"So, you have noticed that too," Itilakna said with a smile in his voice.

"Should I ask the reverend to explain to me about the sad man?" Minko said sleepily.

"Please do not, Son, for I fear that if you do, the Reverend Grant will feel he must explain it all. He is a great talker, and we might be here for days." Minko Ushi giggled at his father's joke and fell asleep smiling.

Chapter Ten

They rose early and ate cold leftovers for breakfast. The Reverend Grant gave the travelers the rest of the ham and bread to take with them.

"I wish you Godspeed, Itilakna. Have you decided if you will cross the river with us, or will you walk on this side and try to catch a ride somewhere farther upriver?"

"We will cross the river now, and then walk. It is many miles shorter, and there is no assurance that we will find a ride farther up the river," Itilakna said, shaking the reverend's outstretched hand.

They walked down to the small dock and loaded the last of the things from the church onto the boat. Minko Ushi had to cover Black Spot's eyes to get him on the boat, for the pony did not like it any better than Minko did.

"It will be fine, Black Spot," he whispered in the horse's

flickering ear. "We are only crossing the river. It won't take any time at all."

"There is a landing dock about three miles from here, on the west side of the river. You can pick up the trail there, but it's hard traveling, even in good weather," the Reverend Grant said.

"I have been warned about the dangers, but we have no choice. We must continue," Itilakna said.

Once they got under way, it took only a short time for Jacob to navigate the low river, avoiding the sandbars and hidden rocks skillfully. Black Spot and Minko stayed near the rail, but this time the boy didn't feel sick, for which he was grateful.

When the landing dock came into sight, Jacob maneuvered the boat into a wide half-circle. He came alongside the dock and let down the ramp. Black Spot scrambled around on the wet deck and was down the ramp and running across the snow-covered ground before Minko Ushi and his father could even gather their belongings. He was out of sight by the time the boat pulled away.

"Godspeed, my friends," the reverend called, waving from the deck of the boat. Minko and Itilakna returned the wave and then turned their backs on the river and began the long walk to Fort Smith.

The weather was cold and windy, but the skies were clear. The territory west of the river was wild and dangerous, so most people traveled by water. Though they had been warned of the huge swamps and dense forests they would encounter, nothing could have prepared them for what they found.

There was a trail, but it was so overgrown and rocky, it was nearly impossible to follow. The trees were a solid wall on both sides of the path, and sometimes Itilakna had to use his big hunting knife to hack a way through the thick tangle of undergrowth. The snow had drifted into huge piles against the rocky hills, and Minko had to follow his father through these freezing mountains of snow, fighting to hold his footing and not fall too far behind.

Before the day was done, he felt the familiar numbness in his feet and knew that they were beginning to freeze. He said nothing to his father because he did not want to be the cause of a delay. By late afternoon he was exhausted from fighting the snow and the tangles of dead vegetation. Still he said nothing, though he fell farther and farther behind.

Just before sunset, his father called a halt for the day. The trees that had caused them so much grief now provided them with excellent shelter from the winter winds and with wood for a comforting fire.

While his father cut ham and bread, Minko stretched out near the fire and clenched his teeth against the pain when his feet began to thaw. He unwrapped the leather strips, took his frozen moccasins off, and wrapped his feet in the bearskin. He didn't want his father to see his pain and did his best to hide it.

They ate their food in silence, and Minko soon fell into an exhausted sleep. He woke once in the night to see his father working on their leather leggings and moccasins by the light of the fire. He fell asleep again and dreamed of blue skies and warm summer days.

Itilakna woke Minko early next morning. "Let me look at your feet, Son. I need to see if you have suffered any permanent damage."

So, Minko thought, I did not fool him at all.

"They look fine to me," Itilakna said. "Do your toes hurt?"

"No, Father. They burned like fire last night, but they are fine now," Minko answered sleepily.

"Good. I have made you new moccasins and wraps for your feet. Your mother would never forgive me if I brought you back to her with your toes missing. You would never be allowed to go anywhere with me again," Itilakna said, grinning at his son.

Minko Ushi nodded. "You are right, Father. She can be fearsome when she is angry."

As they were preparing to leave, Minko said, "I wonder why Black Spot has not caught up with us."

"It is more likely we have not caught up with him," Itilakna said as he shouldered his bundle. Minko thought about that for a while and decided his father was right. Black Spot always appeared when he was ready to be a pet again, or a packhorse.

"Father, if Black Spot is in front of us, how does he know which way to go? Why does he never get lost?" he asked.

"That horse of yours is a mystery to me. I almost believe that he would have followed us to the Territory on his own, if we had not taken him with us."

"Perhaps he is a spirit horse. A gift from the horse tribe, sent to watch over us," Minko said quietly.

"It could be so," Itilakna said, "but he acts more like a human than a spirit."

At midday, there was still no sign of Black Spot, and a forest of cane stalks was directly ahead. Though a trail had once been cut through the canebrake, it had become overgrown, and once again Itilakna had to cut a new trail. The stubs of the cane were tough and made walking difficult; the soft moccasins offered little protection.

When they stopped for the night, there was still no end in sight. The cane seemed to go on forever. With feet sore and bruised, they cleared a small space and used the cane to build a fire. They ate the rest of the ham and bread, laid the bearskin on the frozen ground, and covered up with the two blankets the reverend had given them. Both were asleep before the sun was fully set.

The next day passed exactly like the first, with no time and no energy for talking. Minko was afraid that they would never get out of the canebrake, and he hated the idea of spending another night trying to sleep on the cane stubs. By late afternoon, he could see that even his father's great strength was being drained by the constant need to clear a trail with the knife.

Just at sunset, when Minko was sure he couldn't take another step, they were suddenly out of the cane. Before them lay a vast, snow-covered meadow, and a mile or so to the south, a great forest of oak and cedar trees.

Though their way was to be across the meadow, Itilakna put his arm around his son's shoulder and walked with him toward the trees. They set up camp and huddled beside the fire, eating cold jerky and trying to get warm.

"I am getting worried about Black Spot, Father," Minko said. "There are things in this new place that are dangerous for such a little pony."

"I am sure he is fine, Minko. He is much too smart to be caught by any bear or wildcat."

"What about wolves? They are probably having a hard time finding food, just as we are. They might think he is a deer."

"The wolves must have heard you, Son. I think we have company," Itilakna said, looking into the darkness over his son's shoulder.

Minko turned around slowly and stared into the trees. At first he saw nothing, but as his eyes adjusted, he saw the wolves. Two large, dark shapes were sitting there, watching them.

"What are they doing, Father?" he asked quietly.

"I cannot say, Son. They are not afraid, or they wouldn't be sitting, and they aren't hunting us, or they would be better hidden."

"Could it be that they are just curious, like the wildcats?" Minko asked.

"If it is only the two of them, that is most likely the case. But if there are more of them somewhere out there in the darkness, then it may mean trouble."

"What should we do, Father?"

"Nothing, for now. It is they who will decide what is to be done."

"I was tired and ready to sleep, but now I am wide awake," Minko said.

"Good. Then you may take the first watch, and I will get some sleep. Keep your eyes and ears open and wake me at once if they start moving this way, or if you see more of them."

Minko stared at Itilakna in amazement. "You are going to trust me to guard you while you sleep?"

"Of course. If I cannot trust you with my life, who may I

trust? Wake me when you are sleepy, and I will take over. Good night, Son."

Itilakna lay down on the bearskin, turned his back to the fire and Minko, and settled in to sleep. Minko looked back at the two wolves, but they remained as they had been. What do I do now? he wondered. He decided he needed to build up the fire, because most animals are afraid of fire. Maybe that would scare them away. Once the fire was burning brightly, he checked to make sure the rifle was nearby, and then he sat down and he and the wolves watched one another.

A few minutes later, he thought he heard something off to his left, but when he looked around he couldn't see or hear anything. He looked back to the wolves just in time to see them fading away into the darkness. It make him a little nervous that he couldn't see them anymore. Were they still watching from a different place? Had they met up with the others from their pack, and were they getting ready to attack? Calling on all his courage, he walked to the edge of the circle of light and began walking its perimeter. If the wolves were going to come, he had to be on his feet, ready to act.

Round and round he went. After a while he began to relax. If they were coming, they would have done so by now. He put some more wood on the fire and sat down.

Some time later he jerked his head up and realized instantly that he had been sleeping. And standing in front of him, less than twenty feet away, was a wolf.

They stared at each other, boy and wolf, and Minko saw that the intruder was all legs and ears. A pup! he thought. The wolf is just a pup. Where were his parents? Minko quickly scanned

the darkness beyond the camp but saw and heard nothing. The wolf pup was still staring at Minko and then, as if making a decision, walked a few feet closer.

Should I wake Father? he wondered. The wolf and the boy stared at one another. No, he decided, I can take care of this myself. There was something about the wolf's look that reminded Minko of Black Spot. He recognized that look.

Keeping his eyes on the wolf pup, he felt around for the supply pouch, found it, and took out some jerky. He threw the jerky as hard as he could in the direction of the wolf, and the wolf pup wheeled around and ran. Stopping a few yards away, he turned around and looked at Minko reproachfully. Then he raised his nose into the air and began sniffing. He caught the scent of the dried meat, put his nose to the snow-covered ground, and followed it to the jerky. He looked once more at Minko, grabbed the jerky, and ran clumsily back the way he had come.

"Well done, Son," Itilakna said quietly.

"Aahh!" Minko shouted, jumping to his feet as he spun around. He had forgotten all about his father for a moment, and now he felt his face growing hot with shame for squealing like a frightened puppy.

Ignoring Minko's reaction, Itilakna asked, "What made you offer food instead of using the rifle?"

"I have seen that same look on Black Spot's face when he's hungry, so I made a peace offering, and the wolf accepted it," Minko said, struggling to regain his calm.

"You constantly surprise me with your wisdom, little one," Itilakna said, smiling at his son. "Now, why don't you get some sleep, and I will take the next watch, though I do not think we have to worry about the wolves any longer."

"Good night, Father," Minko said, suddenly very tired. The wolves did not return.

They started across the snowy meadow just after sunup. The traveling was easier, but still the snow cover and the treacherous trail slowed them. Early in the evening of the fifth day they set up camp beside a tiny stream that flowed in spite of the frigid temperatures. Itilakna had managed to take two rabbits that day, so while their evening meal cooked over a hot fire, they set up a shelter. Itilakna had decided they would spend the next day hunting and resting, so that they could complete the last part of their journey with a minimum of delay.

As the night closed in, the silence of their frozen world was shattered by the sound of gunfire. Minko found it hard to place the direction of the sound, but clearly it was very near. One shot and then another echoed through the hills.

Itilakna grabbed his rifle and, pulling Minko by the hand, ran away from the campfire and into the darkness. He heard two audible clicks that could only be a firing pin striking an empty chamber. Whoever it was, he was out of bullets.

"Stay behind me, Minko, and be very quiet," Itilakna whispered. There was no need to tell Minko to be quiet, for his heart was pounding in his chest and he couldn't have spoken even if he had wanted to. Suddenly a man stumbled into their camp, cradling a rifle in his arms. He looked around wildly and spotted the cooking rabbits. He seemed not to know or care that there might be danger. Dropping to his knees, he reached for the food, letting his rifle fall to the ground.

Itilakna moved so fast, Minko had no time to react. He watched as his father stood before the man.

"Stop," Itilakna said in English. The man, dressed in a long fur coat, a fur hat, and army boots, froze for a moment and then looked up at the rifle pointing at him. Still looking at the rifle, the man started feeling in the snow for his own gun.

"It will do you no good," Itilakna said quietly. "You are out of bullets."

The stranger stood up slowly and looked at Itilakna. As he did, Minko saw the bearded face in the firelight and caught his breath. Itilakna too recognized the face of Wagon Master Timmons.

"Well, well," Timmons said. "If it ain't one of the poor injuns. I figured you'd all be dead by now, what with the sickness and all." Itilakna said nothing. As they stared at one another, Timmons began to fidget, moving his hands and looking away from the huge Indian who stood so silently.

"Look here, will ya? I'm on my way back to Memphis from Fort Smith. My horse pulled up lame a couple days ago, and then ran away in the night with most of my supplies and all my ammunition. I just used my last two bullets, tryin' to kill somethin' to eat. I can't go back to Fort Smith 'cause they ain't too happy with me there, so I got no choice but to keep goin'."

Itilakna did not speak but continued to point his rifle at Timmons's head. "Well," the man said nervously, "the long and short of it is, I ain't ate for two days, and I'm likely to die out here if I don't get some food and ammunition."

Itilakna stared at the red-bearded face for a moment and finally spoke. "I do not like you, Timmons, but if you had asked, I would have given you food."

"Weren't nobody around, or I woulda asked. Anyways, I'm askin' now. Could you spare me a bite?"

Itilakna motioned the man away from the fire with his rifle and called Minko. Minko came quickly and his father said, "Get his rifle, Son, and bring it to me." Minko did as his father said and handed the gun over, being careful to stay out of the man's reach.

"Sit, Timmons, and I will share our food," Itilakna said, lowering his rifle. They ate in silence, and when Minko drifted off to sleep, both men were still awake. He knew that neither trusted the other, and that neither would sleep this night.

Minko woke suddenly at dawn to find Timmons gone and Itilakna stirring the fire to life.

"Where has he gone, Father?"

"To Memphis, I hope. I gave him a flint rock, dry bark, and some of the government rations."

"Did you give him bullets for his gun?" Minko asked worriedly.

"Yes, I did. I gave him four bullets, because he could not survive without the gun. I do not think he will bother us again."

"Why did you help him? He would have left us to die, if things were the other way around," Minko said indignantly.

"So," Itilakna said quietly, "you would have me act like him?"

"No," Minko said, "I would not want that, but it seems wrong to help someone who wishes us dead."

"I think it is going to bother Timmons very much to know

that, for always, he will owe his life to me, a Chata." Itilakna smiled, and Minko smiled too, suddenly realizing that his father had pulled off a great coup! He could have killed the man but instead had embarrassed him for all time. It made Minko feel like dancing and laughing and shouting at the sky. So he did. And Itilakna laughed and slapped his knees and shouted war cries into the freezing air.

Chapter Eleven

Seven days later they reached Fort Smith, just after sundown. Freezing and exhausted, they were directed to Major F. W. Armstrong, the new Choctaw agent. He was in Fort Smith trying to gather supplies for the thousands of Indians soon to arrive. Major Armstrong told them the new agency was a half-day's walk, southwest of Fort Smith.

"Welcome to Indian Territory, Itilakna," Major Armstrong said. "We will have the wagons loaded in another half hour, and you're welcome to ride along with us back to the agency."

"You will drive the road at night?" Itilakna asked.

"Yes. Well, we have a schedule to keep, you know. The roads are in fair shape now, but if it snows again, we'll be stuck. Best to go while we can," Major Armstrong said. Minko Ushi could tell that the major was not used to having his decisions questioned.

"We will ride with the major," Itilakna told his son. Minko's feet hurt, and he was so tired he didn't want to move. The major's little office was warm, and Minko was beginning to feel sleepy. He didn't much care what they did, as long as he didn't have to walk in the snow anymore.

If it had been warmer, the road would have been impossible to travel, but the mud was frozen solid. The wagons jerked and wobbled across the deep trenches. Itilakna and Minko rode atop the seed-corn sacks, and Minko was sure that he would not be able to sleep through the bone-jarring ride. Talking was also impossible, so they rode in silence.

Since the moon was full, the major's decision to travel at night was not entirely foolhardy. Minko pulled back the flaps and held on to them so he wouldn't be thrown out. They were in the first wagon, so all Minko could see out the flap was the team of horses pulling the second wagon. Big and sturdy, they plodded along with their heads down. They are as tired and sleepy as I am, Minko thought. He wanted to ask his father about Black Spot. They had not seen the little pony once since crossing the Arkansas River. But he decided to wait until they reached the agency.

Just after midnight Minko was awakened by the stillness. They had stopped moving and his father was gone. Scrambling across the corn sacks, he could feel the fear churning his stomach. Pulling back the canvas flaps, he saw his father and took a deep breath of relief. Itilakna was helping to unload the second wagon.

The big storehouse was made of rough logs. There were lamps everywhere, and soldiers and civilians went about the business of unloading the wagons as quickly as possible.

Large hands reached up and lifted him down from the wagon. "Down ya come, lad," said a man of medium height with hair as black as Minko's own and twinkling blue eyes. "Your father decided to let you sleep, though it beats me how you could sleep on that road," he said, grinning at Minko. The grin was contagious, and Minko found himself smiling broadly. He liked the man instantly. Itilakna came just then and said to Minko, "Go inside, Son, and stay warm." The man stuck out his hand, and Minko took it, as he had seen white men do. They shook hands, and Minko felt he had made his first friend in this new place.

They were allowed to sleep on the floor of the new agency building, which stood next to the storehouse. Minko slept soundly, and Major Armstrong greeted them warmly when he arrived the next morning. "Come, share my breakfast. I would be happy to have you join me." Though the major spoke no Choctaw, Itilakna understood the invitation and pulled Minko along to the major's table.

"You're very lucky, Itilakna. Since you are among the first to arrive, you have your choice of building sites, as well as most of the supplies you will need to get started," the major said as he cut into his pancakes. Minko Ushi saw his father look at the major the way he had looked at Jacob Speers. The major must have remembered that he was speaking to a man who had lost everything, for he added hastily, "Well, perhaps 'lucky' is not the right word."

"Is there any news of my people?" Itilakna asked.

"I had a report three days ago that they had arrived at Arkansas Post but were stranded there. The river was low and partially frozen, and they couldn't navigate the channel. They are camped there now, waiting for the river to rise. They weathered the storm with only a few casualties, but I have heard that there is much sickness." Itilakna said nothing but got up and walked out the door.

Minko hurried out behind him, taking one last bite of pancake with him. Together they walked to the storehouse, where their supplies were being loaded onto a wagon. Shovels, a crosscut saw, pickaxes, nails and hammers, cooking pots, a plow and one extra blade, lamps and coal oil, a tent for temporary shelter, one horse, and what was supposed to be a six-month supply of corn, dried beef, flour and cornmeal, salt and salt pork, and seed corn for spring planting. Itilakna and the supply agent worked quickly, and Minko stayed out of the way.

"Little brother," said a Choctaw voice, "does this pony know you?" Minko turned around, and there stood Black Spot, a rope around his neck, held by a smiling young man from his village.

Not wanting to appear childish, Minko forced himself to stay calm. "Yes, that is my pony, Black Spot. Where did you find him?"

"He found me. My friends and I have been here for some time now, and this pony came two days ago, begging for food. Did he run away?"

"I guess he did not want to ride on any more boats, so he came ahead of us." Black Spot was rubbing his muzzle in Minko's hair. He snorted softly, ignoring Minko's attempts to push him away. The young man laughed and handed over the rope. "Well, I can see that he belongs to you."

Itilakna had finished loading the wagon. When he walked toward his son and saw who was speaking to him, he started to laugh. It made Minko smile just to hear his father laugh again.

"Nashoba Nowa! So you have found your way to the Territory. Where is the rest of the lost party?"

"I see that we are never to hear the end of this, Itilakna," Nashoba Nowa said, shaking his head in regret.

"Do not feel bad, Nashoba. You have learned a valuable lesson. If Jackson's government offers you something, look for hidden flaws before you accept it."

"I think all of the Chata have learned that lesson, Itilakna."

"Nashoba Nowa," Minko said, pulling on the young man's shirt. "Thank you for taking care of my pony."

"It was my pleasure, little brother. He is quite a pony, you know."

"I believe he is a very special horse, sent to watch over me. It's just that he hasn't learned to do that job very well," Minko said, rubbing the little pony's head. Nashoba nodded in agreement, and then he spoke to Itilakna again.

"We are nearly finished with our cabins. As soon as we are done, we will come and help you. There is some good land near us. Come, let me show you."

They tied the new horse to the back of the wagon, and Black Spot trotted along behind. Minko kept a sharp eye on the little pony, just in case he should decide to leave again. The sun came out for a while, and it seemed a little warmer, but the snow cover here was even deeper than on the trail behind them. They passed Nashoba's cabin just before midday, and shortly after that the wagon driver stopped under the bare branches of an ancient oak tree.

"I know you cannot tell much about the land under all this

snow, but there is good water on the other side of those trees, and not too many rocks to be removed," Nashoba said.

Itilakna looked out over the land with a practiced eye. There was an open meadow that would not take much clearing, and a good stand of trees for firewood, and logs for building.

"Yes, Nashoba, it does look good," Itilakna said. "Let's unload the supplies. We will build here." Minko could see no difference between this land and any other, but he trusted his father's judgment. So, he thought, I am home.

"Come and stay with us, Itilakna," Nashoba was saying. "Wait until we can come and help you."

"I wouldn't leave this stuff here," the wagon driver said. "Buncha thievin' white trash movin' in like vultures, stealin' everythin' that ain't nailed down." It was hard to see what the driver looked like, because he was wrapped in bearskin with a muffler across the bottom half of his face. Itilakna thanked him for the warning and then turned to his young friend.

"I will stay here, Nashoba, but I thank you for your offer of shelter."

"I think that after what you and the young one have been through, this will not be difficult for you. But should you change your mind, you are welcome to come to my home, such as it is."

"Come on, Walking Wolf, I'll give you a ride back up the road," the driver said, using Nashoba Nowa's English name.

As soon as the wagon was turned around, Itilakna set about getting organized. "First thing to do is get the tent set up," he told Minko. This proved to be an exhausting, time-consuming job, because all Itilakna knew of army tents was what he had seen in Memphis. After much grumbling and muttering, he got the tent to stand, but it looked strangely tilted.

Itilakna finally threw up his hands and said, "That will have to do. I can do no more with this thing."

Minko had been busily gathering wood and building a fire, and feeding Black Spot and the new horse from the sack of oats the driver had thrown off. When he looked up and saw the sad-looking tent, he slapped his hand across his mouth to keep from giggling out loud.

Itilakna came to the fire and saw his son struggling not to laugh. "What is so funny?" he demanded. Minko pointed to the tent and the laughter came rolling out. Itilakna looked at the droopy, tilted tent and laughed in spite of himself.

And so began the hard work of rebuilding a life. For the next few weeks they lived much as they had along the trail. Itilakna took one day a week to hunt. He found that if he hung the meat in the trees, it would freeze and still be protected from predators. Game was scarce, but with the corn and dried beef, they had enough to eat.

The work of cutting logs for the cabin was hard at the best of times, but in the freezing snow, it was doubly difficult. Minko helped when his father used the crosscut, a long saw blade with a handle at both ends, operated by pushing and pulling the blade through the tree. Itilakna used the new horse and Black Spot, when he was willing, to haul the logs one by one from the woods to the cabin site. Their new home was to be well back from the road, close to the little stream.

Minko Ushi knew he wasn't much help, so he was glad when Nashoba showed up with some of his friends. "Itilakna, who set your tent up?" Nashoba said as he and the other young men laughed at the lopsided tent.

"Since you are so smart, Nashoba, perhaps you can put it right," Itilakna replied, unhooking the horses. Nashoba's three friends cheerfully fixed the tent, with much laughing and talking. Then they all went into the woods to cut more logs, and Minko set about the task of cooking a midday meal for his father's friends. By sunset the log pile had grown considerably, and with promises of help for tomorrow, the young men left.

"I think that two or three more days of logging will give us enough to start putting up the cabin," Itilakna said as they entered the tent for the night.

"Look, Father, there is much more room in here now," Minko said, looking around. "But all the same, I am ready to be in a real home again. I just wish Mother and my grandparents were here. I know it is hard for them, because it has been hard for us."

"I know, Son. I am getting very worried that it is taking so long to get them here. I only hope that they are someplace dry and warm."

"Sometimes I dream of them, and they always look well, so I am sure they are, Father."

"Let us hope your dreams are true, Son. Good night."

"Good night, Father."

Four days later, Itilakna assigned Minko the task of notching the logs. Since the ground was frozen and there was no mud to use as sealer, each log had to be notched so that it would lock together with the next. Sealing the cracks would have to wait until the spring.

When the cabin was about halfway up, Itilakna and Minko

Ushi had to go to the agency and ask for replacement tools and more corn. Ax handles had broken, the saw blade had dulled and would not sharpen, and the corn given them as food was moldy and rotting.

Itilakna found Major Armstrong, who had to call for an interpreter because he could not understand Itilakna's angry words.

"I regret that you are having problems, but we have kept our side of the bargain. We cannot be responsible if you abuse your tools or allow the corn to get wet and moldy."

"I have grown corn all my life, Major. That corn rotted from the bottom up. You allowed it to get wet on the bottom and kept it instead of throwing it away or drying it out," Itilakna said angrily. "The metal in the tools is inferior, the wood in the handles knotted and weak. I want decent tools, Major, a fair replacement for the ones I was forced to leave behind. I want dry corn, Major, and you will give it to me."

"Itilakna, what we have in storage is for the rest of the people, who will be coming along soon. I simply cannot replace tools because you say they are inferior. You people are going to have to learn to take better care of the things you're given. As for the corn, you may come back in two months and pick up another three-month supply. Now, good day, sir."

Itilakna watched the major walk away, and Minko Ushi saw his father's anger boiling over.

"It does not matter, Father," he said. "We do not need their help."

"It is just as the elders said, Minko. You cannot trust the government. They are men without honor."

When they returned home, they found Nashoba and two young men putting the logs together. He told his friends of the encounter with the major. Nashoba nodded and said, "I should have warned you about the major. We ran into some of the same problems, but the major would not help us either. We were hoping things would go better for you."

"How did you finish your homes?"

"We made new handles for the axes, and worked harder and sharpened the saw blades more often. It was slow, hard work, but there was nothing else to do."

"Then that is what I must do, but it makes me very angry. I do not like liars or cheats."

"If we help each other, we will be fine. The less we depend on the government, the better off we will be," Nashoba said.

It took until the next new moon to finish the cabin, but at last it was done. Itilakna built a smaller copy of the fireplace from the little cabin that had provided them shelter, and though it was a lot of extra work, he was very pleased when it was done. It looked much like the old cabin at home, but it had two separate sleeping rooms instead of one.

"You mean one of the rooms is to be mine?" Minko had never thought to be happy again, but seeing the new cabin built and having his own room thrilled him. He had helped build this place, and he took a great deal of pride in that. He wanted his mother and grandparents to hurry and come to this new home.

Hvsh Chvfó Chitó, the Month of Big Hunger, came, and with it sleet and snow and a terrible, howling wind, and still there was no word. They managed to put up a shelter for Black Spot and the new horse. Itilakna was forced to hunt in the worst weather so that they would have enough to eat. And in the hearts of the man and boy, dark fear came to stay.

Chapter Twelve

When the weather cleared,
Minko helped his father put up storage bins for the corn crop
they hoped to have by late summer. The seed corn was still
good, and the grandparents carried with them squash, pump-
kin, and gourd seeds. The coming of the next full moon sig-
naled the start of Hvshi Máhli, the Wind Month. Now the
ground could be worked and the planting could begin.

One day in Hvshi Máhli they worked steadily until the sun
was high in the sky before Itilakna called a halt. They had started
to walk back to the cabin when the unmistakable sound of
army wagons made them both break into a run. A wagon was
pulling up under the big oak tree, and from out of the back
came Mother.

Itilakna ran to her and wrapped her in his big arms. She
clung to him and began to cry.

"Help your grandfather," she said, pushing herself away

from her husband. She turned to find Minko standing quietly, with tears running down his face. She held out her arms and dropped to her knees, and he threw himself at her.

"Oh, Mother, I was so afraid you would never come," he sobbed into her shoulder. She smoothed back his hair and kissed his face and smiled at him through her own tears.

"I said I would come, little one, and so I have. Only the thought of you and your father kept me going. Otherwise I would surely have died." Itilakna came to them with his arm around his grandfather's shoulder. Minko Ushi was shocked by the old man's appearance. The once bright, cheerful face was sunken, and he was so thin that he looked like a walking skeleton. The tall frame, once as erect as his grandson's, was now bent, and he trembled so badly he needed a stick to help him walk.

Itilakna's grandmother was not in the wagon, and Minko knew in his heart that she was gone, for she would never have left her husband's side. But hope will not die on its own; it must be killed. And as the wagon pulled away, Itilakna asked, "Where are your parents, my love? Did you get separated? And what of my grandmother?"

"We need to get Grandfather into the house. Then we will talk," Mother said in a small voice.

"How do you like the new cabin, Mother? I helped build it, you know," Minko said.

"You did a fine job, Son. I am very proud of you," Mother said, but she barely looked at the cabin as they made their way inside. Minko knew he did not want to hear what Mother was about to say, but he had to face her news like a man. If she could live through it, then he could hear about it.

They put Grandfather on a pallet near the fireplace and covered him up with blankets. Mother dipped soup out of the pot and lifted the old man's head to feed him. After three or four bites, he closed his eyes, sighed deeply, and fell into sleep. Only then would she accept a bowl of corn soup from her husband, but she did not eat.

Minko looked carefully at his mother and saw that she had grown very thin and looked much older than he remembered. Her dress was stained and torn and, worst of all, there were deep cuts and scratches on her arms and legs. They were fiery red and leaked thick yellow pus.

She took a shaky breath and began to speak, staring into the fire. "The rain in Memphis flooded the river valleys, and we could not travel to Arkansas Post in wagons as the soldiers had planned. We had to wait in the rain and cold for boats.

"They packed us onto two boats, and we came to Arkansas Post. But the boats were needed by the soldiers, and they left us there. By this time, my mother and your grandmother were both sick. It hurt them to breathe, and they stopped asking for food. Their skin was as hot as that fire," she said, nodding at the blaze in the fireplace. "I used up the few plants we had brought with us to make medicine for them, and when it was gone, the fever was back worse than ever. We were at Arkansas Post for two weeks, and that is when the storm struck. Because of a mix-up, and the bad weather, twenty-five hundred Chata from the Northwestern District were taken to the Post and left there. There were sixty tents to shelter all of us. It wasn't nearly enough. It was just like Memphis, only the temperature dropped, and the wind howled and the snow piled up, and we had no clothes, few blankets, and after five days, only half-rations."

She looked up at her husband and tears filled her dark, sad eyes. "We waited for boats, but the river was iced over. My mother died in a wagon on the way to Little Rock. I did not even know when she slipped away, Itilakna. Your grandmother died in a leaky, freezing tent soon after we reached Little Rock. She held my hand and said, 'Tell my grandson that he must come for me and give me a proper burial at our new home.' Your *amofo*, your grandfather, sang his own death song then, willing himself to die. He has very nearly succeeded," she said, looking at the sunken face of the sleeping old man.

Itilakna took her small hands in his and looked into her eyes. "I have no words to comfort you, my love. I only know that I love you, and that if I could take the hurt away, I would gladly give my life." She smiled, a sad little smile, and squeezed his hands gently.

"Their bodies lie in a storage building in Little Rock," she continued. "The soldiers said there was not enough room in the wagons for the living, much less the dead. They buried many people beside the trail, but the ground was frozen in Little Rock, so our dead lie waiting to come home. The soldiers said they would send the bodies to us in the spring."

"What of your father?" Itilakna asked softly.

"Oh, Itilakna, I do not know!" Mother whispered. "He was in the wagon when we started to Fort Smith, but he was nowhere to be found when we arrived. When we stopped to rest for the last time, I could not find him. He is gone, and I do not know how or why."

"Then there is hope," Itilakna said. "In his grief, he may have just wanted to be alone. He may show up at the door at any moment." Mother said nothing, but it was clear, even to Minko, that she did not believe it.

As Minko listened to his mother, the tears rolled down his cheeks unnoticed. He felt his mother's sorrow as if it were a living thing. It engulfed him and became a part of him, and he did not try to push it away. They sat in silence until Mother spoke again.

"I met your friend John Turner," she said. "He came looking for us, and when he saw how it was at Little Rock, he bundled us up and took us to his place. I think it is only because of him that your grandfather still lives." She put her arm around Minko and smiled down at him. "He spoke very highly of you, little Minko, and of your father. He returned many times to that miserable camp and brought back as many of our people as his stable would hold. He fed us and doctored us, and there are many who owe their lives to him." Her tears flowed as she continued her story. "He cried when he saw the children, and he gathered them up and found clothes and shoes for those who had none. He could not save them all, and they died, Itilakna. Tiny newborns, toddlers, and little ones all died, and John Turner cursed his God and his government, and he cried until he had no tears left to cry." Itilakna hung his head, and Minko saw that his father wept.

His mother slept then, wrapped in her husband's arms, too sad and too tired to go on.

The next day, his mother slept on, waking only long enough to eat a little soup before falling to sleep again. Minko sat beside his sleeping great-grandfather's bed, holding his cold hand and telling him of the journey he and Itilakna had made.

"You would have been proud of him, *Amofo*. You taught him well, and because of him, we survived a journey that killed many of our people. You survived too, Grandfather, and now you can teach me the things you taught my father. You must not leave me. I have lost too much already. Please wake up, *Amofo,* and say you will stay." The old man lay silent, giving no sign that he had heard his great-grandson.

Itilakna came into the house, having just returned from Nashoba's house. "How is he doing, Son?" he asked, stamping his feet to shake off the snow.

"He will be fine," Minko said. "He just needs to rest, and soon he will be his old, funny self."

"Nashoba says none of them brought any medicine, but he will ask around. He did have some sassafras root, so we can make some tea."

"Father, what of Nashoba's family?" Minko asked, dreading to hear but needing to know.

Itilakna shook his head and said, "His mother and father made it, but his grandfather died last night."

"But he was the storyteller, the keeper of their family history, just as my *amofo* is. What will happen, Father, if there is no one to carry on?"

"All of their history will be lost, because Nashoba's uncle, who was learning the stories from his father, is also dead."

"Do you hear that, Grandfather?" Minko said, turning back

to the unconscious old man. "Remember when you said that I would be the storyteller one day? You must stay until you can tell me the stories." There was no response.

"He has been a stubborn old man, putting off your learning because he thought you were too young. Now I fear it may be too late," Itilakna said.

"I have asked the Great Father to spare *Amofo*. But I think it is up to him whether he will stay or go, so I have been talking to him."

"That can do no harm, and it may be that he can hear, wherever he is, and will heed you." Itilakna smiled at his son.

Several days later, as Itilakna tried patiently to feed his unconscious grandfather, the old man's eyes suddenly opened and looked straight into the face of his grandson.

"Who do you call stubborn, Itilakna?" the old man asked in a dry, croaking voice. Minko was sitting near the fireplace, trying to string the new bow he had made. He heard the familiar voice and went flying to Grandfather, throwing himself on the bony chest of the old man. "*Amofo,* you will not die?" he asked as he laid his head over his great-grandfather's heart.

"No, no, little Minko," the old man said, stroking the dark head. "I was just resting. Gathering my strength. I thank you for talking to me, keeping me company while I was away. And now, little one, if you would remove yourself from my chest, so that I may continue to breathe."

Itilakna's smile lit up the room. Minko Ushi watched as his father struggled for words.

"Grandfather, I do not know how to say . . . ," he stammered.

The old man patted his grandson's arm and said, "The smile

on your face says all I need to know. Now, help me sit up and give me that soup."

In the weeks that followed, Grandfather grew strong, and though he no longer wished to die, the marks of the death march clung to him. As soon as he was strong enough, he began to teach Minko the family stories, the legends, and the history. It was important that each story be in its correct place and each legend remembered word for word. There was much for Minko to learn and he set about the task happily.

As the days passed, the boy began to wonder why Mother seldom wanted to do anything. She sat quietly in the rocker made for her by her husband, staring at the wall or sleeping.

One day Itilakna sat down beside Grandfather while the old man was instructing Minko Ushi on the proper way to sharpen a hunting knife. "I am very worried about my wife, Grandfather," he said. "The wounds on her body are healing, but I cannot see the healing of her heart. She is so very sad, and though she walks and talks to me, my wife is not here."

"Death has touched her, Grandson, and now she cannot be free of it. Her spirit has been assaulted and lies bleeding and torn inside her. If she is not strong enough, it will be her death we mourn next." Minko listened to the men's words and fear gripped his heart.

"No, Grandfather," Itilakna whispered. "I could not bear it if I lost her. It is she who helps me keep my place in the world. Now she sits in her chair and stares at nothing. What can I do to help her?"

"You can do nothing but what you do now, which is to love her. She must fight this battle alone, against the greatest enemy any of us will ever face, and that is a broken spirit."

"I feel helpless. I cannot see an enemy to fight, yet I cannot sit by and watch her slip away from me," Itilakna said, getting up to pace the room, his big hands clenched into fists.

"Let go of the anger and hatred you feel for the people who caused this. It will poison you, and you will not be any help to your wife," Grandfather said, reading Itilakna's face perfectly.

"How did you know what I was thinking?" Itilakna asked.

"Because, when your grandmother died, I felt the same anger and hatred. I wanted a war club and skulls to smash. I wanted to see this great chief, Jackson, and look into his eyes as he died by my hand. I still feel that way, but it is useless, and I will not pollute my soul with poisonous anger over something I cannot change."

Minko listened to Grandfather speak and felt a great wave of love for the wise old man. Though his body was old and bent, his great spirit shone out of the sparkling black eyes.

"It is a good thing you did not leave me, old man," Itilakna said. "I would surely have died of my own foolishness."

"That is the truth you speak, *ippok naki,* my grandson." The old man grinned at him. "Now, go see if you can get your wife interested in living. Give her work to do, something to care about again. Perhaps," he said, "a baby?"

"We have always wanted other children, but it seems as if it is not to be," Itilakna said, shaking his head. "And now, with her so sad, it is even less likely. A woman who is to be a new mother must want her child, and my wife wants nothing."

Chapter Thirteen

As the weeks went by and the earth roused herself, Itilakna and Minko were busy plowing and planting. Sometimes Minko and Black Spot slipped away to explore their new home ground.

"Mother, Black Spot and I are going to the creek. It is beautiful there. Cool, green, and very much like home. Will you come with us?"

"I do not think so, Minko. I feel tired today. Perhaps some other time."

"Please, Mother. Come with us. You can rest there just as well."

Sighing deeply, Mother said, "Very well, Minko. You have been after me for days, and I am out of excuses."

She came outside and lifted her face to the sun, and Minko's heart leapt with joy to see a tiny smile. She sat on the new green grass and put her feet into the cool water of the creek. Minko glanced at her from time to time as he chased crawdads and splashed water on Black Spot. They stayed there in the dappled shade until it was time to eat, then walked home hand in hand.

"Thank you, Son," she said. "I had forgotten what wonderful medicine the earth can offer the spirit."

After that, Mother came outside nearly every day, and Minko showed her all the special places he had found. She had brought with her the seeds entrusted to her care by the grandparents, and one day she buried her hands in the tilled soil and planted each seed lovingly. After that, she was always outside, cooking and washing and, finally, singing. And she began giving orders again.

"Itilakna, my love, we need a nice big barn. We will have a huge crop this year, and we will need a place to store it. See to it, will you?" she asked sweetly.

"But the tools, they are no good, and we cannot—" Itilakna began, but she cut him off.

"You can do anything, my husband, and Minko and I will help you, won't we, Son?" She looked and sounded so much like her old self that Minko and his father would have promised her the stars, if she had asked.

"Maybe I can try to sharpen the saw blades, Father," Minko said eagerly.

"Or just maybe I could be makin' y'all some new ones," called a familiar voice.

"John! John Turner, can it be you?" Itilakna shouted to the man coming across the yard.

"Can and is," John said, grinning from ear to ear.

Itilakna pounded him on the back, and Minko smiled shyly up at his friend.

Mother came quietly and put her arms around the man who had saved her life and Grandfather's.

"I brought your people home, little lady. Army was fixin' to bury 'em at Little Rock. Just one more promise 'bout to be broken. While I was at it, I packed up my stuff and sold my livery stable, and I'm havin' me one built at Skullyville."

"I cannot begin to thank you, John, for bringing them home," Mother said. Her mouth trembled and the tears spilled over as she hugged him again. "Our dead are very important to us. It is each family's responsibility to see to their dead, and I could not do it. It has been eating at my heart."

The old burial rites had been outlawed and condemned by the Christians many years ago, but Grandfather still remembered, and now he passed that knowledge on to Minko so that it would not be forgotten. They buried their dead on the back of their property. Beginning at the head, six sticks were placed around the right side of each grave, the shortest sticks first. The sticks held a loop for the soul to grab on to, and each stick was a little taller, to aid the soul in pulling itself out of the grave. The spirits, so long imprisoned in the dead bodies, would now be able to free themselves and continue their journey to the land of spirits. Mother was now at peace, and so were the departed souls of the dead women.

The new agency, and the town that sprang up around it, was called Skullyville—a name derived from the Choctaw word for money, *iskuli*. It was so called because the government had promised, in the Treaty of Dancing Rabbit Creek, to pay the Choctaw people an annuity each month for a year, for all they had lost.

Skullyville began to grow quickly, and John Turner soon had a thriving livery and blacksmith shop there. The whites had to pay him cash, but for the Choctaws John would wait until harvest time for payment. Itilakna got his new tools, and fine tools they were too. By the beginning of Hvsh Bíssa, Month of the Blackberry, the barn was built.

The weather and the loss of more than 100 of the 400 people who had traveled from Memphis had prevented the people from carrying out any tribal business. Their struggle to survive, the betrayal by the government, and the need to mourn their dead had kept the families at home.

Now Itilakna sent word that he wanted to have a naming ceremony and a feast day to celebrate their survival and to send blessings to their dead. Response was slow in coming at first, but as the weather warmed, the families began to send word that they were ready to shake off their sadness.

In Hvshi Bíhi, Mulberry Month, they held a meeting at Itilakna's house, and everyone brought food for the evening meal. It was decided to hold the naming ceremony after the next full moon. While the grown-ups discussed their plans for a new meeting place, a stickball field, and a new ceremonial ground, Minko Ushi sampled the food. It was good to be among his people again and hear the familiar talk. The signs of renewed life were encouraging for everyone.

It was also in the month of Hvshi Bíhi that Mother told them her news.

"I am expecting a child," she said, her face shining with happiness. Itilakna let out a war cry and swept her off her feet, spinning her in big circles until she made him stop.

"Will it be a little brother for me?" Minko asked, not sure how he felt about this new event.

"There is no way to know," his mother said. "But boy or girl, the new child will need a big brother to teach it the things only a big brother knows."

"I could do that," he said thoughtfully. "Yes, I could certainly do that."

That night, just before he slept, Minko heard his parents talking. "The baby will come during Hvsh Chvfó Chitó, the Month of Big Hunger," his mother said. "What if the government decides they want this land too? The new baby will die, Itilakna, and I cannot bear another death." His father made comforting sounds and then said, "That will not happen, my love. We were the first to be sent away, so there hasn't been time for other decisions to be made. By the time this child is grown, I think the government will come knocking on our doors again, but for now, we are safe. Now come, let us get some sleep. I want you to get plenty of rest."

Minko lay awake for some time, thinking about what his mother had said. It was true, they were at the mercy of a cruel, greedy government, and at any time they could be forced to march again. It was an unsettling thought, and when he slipped into sleep, he dreamed of the things his mother had endured. As he slept, the tears rolled silently from his eyes.

The trees cloaked themselves in brilliant green and the wild berries bloomed. Now Minko and Black Spot wandered far and wide, locating friends and finding that other friends had not survived. One day, in a grove of ancient pines, Minko built a small fire and burned cedar and sage, asking for the smoke to carry his prayers for his lost friends to the Great Spirit. The little ceremony eased his heart. He felt better afterward, but he knew he would never forget his friends or his old home.

As he and his horse wandered the countryside, he thought that he might grow to love this wild country. There were no swamps here, but there were gently rolling hills and endless forests where a boy could play all day and easily make his way home before dark. Indian Territory was a vast wilderness, and Minko hoped that it would always be so.

One day Mother felt that she needed to go visiting, to offer condolences and talk to her friends. Itilakna was happy to take her. It would be a one-day trip only, so Minko was given the choice of staying or going. He had never been allowed this privilege before, and he was very surprised.

"You mean I do not have to go?" he asked in amazement.

"You have proven yourself to be a young man," his father said, smiling down on his son. "It is time we treated you as such."

"You may stay home with Grandfather, Minko, but do not go near the stream. It is flooded," his mother said. "When you get hungry, warm up the soup I have left for you, but be careful of the fire, and . . ."

"And have a good time," his father said, smiling as he turned his wife gently to the door. She went, looking worriedly over her shoulder at her son. When the wagon was out of sight, Minko went looking for Black Spot. He found him in the flower-covered meadow, munching on the sweet new grass.

"Come on, Black Spot, we have much to do before Mother returns." Black Spot shook his head up and down and continued eating. Minko started across the meadow, heading for Skullyville. Black Spot, seeing that Minko would not play the begging game, caught up with him quickly.

They walked into the little town and headed for John Turner's livery stable. They found John sitting in the shade of a big chestnut tree.

"Well, hello there, young man. Come and sit with me, and have some cold water," John said in Choctaw. "What brings you to town so early in the day?"

"I have a favor to ask of you, friend John," Minko said. "I wish to buy a gift for my mother, and I want to know if you will use your wagon to take it home."

"Well," John said, scratching his graying head, "I could do that. Were you talking about right now? Today?"

"My mother and father have gone visiting, and I want her gift to be there when she returns home tonight."

John grinned at the boy and said, "Well, let's go pick it up." Minko directed John to the supply storehouse, and they went looking for Minko's friend, the man who had shaken his hand on the night he arrived. They found him stacking sacks of corn at the back of the building. He saw John and Minko, and the big, friendly grin Minko remembered lit up his face.

"Hello there, my little friend," he said, wiping his face on his shirtsleeve. "And to what do I owe this pleasure?" Minko told John what he had come for, and John translated.

"This young fella here has heard you have a cookstove you might be willin' to part with."

"Why, it happens I do!" said the man. "It sits back here in a corner, for I have nowhere else to put it. Would you care to see it?"

"Yes, I would," Minko said, trying out his English.

"By the by," the man said to John, "my name is Colin McCarthy, and who might you be?"

"My apologies, young man," John said, sticking out his hand. "My name is John Turner. I own the new livery stable. This here young fella is Minko Ushi. He don't speak English all that well yet, so I kinda help him."

The stove was buried under sacks of seed corn, and when they moved them, Minko was thrilled by what he saw. Though smaller than John's, the stove was still magnificent. It had double oven doors, a water reservoir, and a warming oven. It would need cleaning, but John declared it a good stove.

"Shall we talk price, then, young Minko Ushi?" Colin asked.

"Did you get that, Minko?" John asked.

Minko nodded and pulled from his shirt a small, leather-wrapped package. It was the five-dollar gold piece John had given him, and he offered it shyly to Colin.

Colin took the coin, bit it, rubbed it with his thumb, and then looked at Minko.

"I am happy to say, young Minko, that we have a deal. Let's shake on it." Minko took the outstretched hand and the deal was made.

When Mother returned that evening, she found Nashoba Nowa, John, Colin, and Minko putting the last piece on the stove. After the introductions were made, Minko showed her his gift. John brought in some wood, fired up the stove, and explained how to use it. Mother paid close attention, and Minko watched her face. He could not tell if the gift pleased her or not.

"Do you like it, Mother? I wanted to make your work easier."

"It is the most wonderful thing I have ever seen," she said, hugging her son. "You have very good friends, and I think you should invite them to eat with us, and I will cook on this wonderful new thing you have given me." The invitation was accepted by everyone, and the evening meal was a great success.

The day of the ceremony dawned clear and bright. It was Hvsh Tákkon, Month of the Peach. The sweet-smelling air was like a tonic, and the Chata people began arriving early in the day. Though the names of the dead were never spoken, there were murmured regrets for "your mother" or "your child." The people came on foot, horseback, and wagon, wearing the best clothes they had. For some, these were patched and worn, but scrubbed clean.

The warm air carried the sound of laughter as friends met friends, and there was the smell of delicious food cooking over an open fire. Each family brought food for the table that was set up under the big oak trees. Because the village fire-keeper had not survived the journey, a new firekeeper was selected.

He laid down four logs, pointing to the four directions.

Speaking to the Great Father, he asked that this sacred fire be blessed, and that the people who would make offerings be granted peace in their hearts and relief from their sorrows.

When the fire was burning brightly, the naming ceremony began. Minko and five other boys were about to receive the first of many names they would have during the course of their adult lives. First the boys went around the table and took a little food from each of the dishes. Then, moving clockwise around the fire, the six boys, from oldest to youngest, made their food offering to the fire and sent their prayers to the spirits of those they had lost. They returned one by one to stand before Grandfather.

The elder of each family would normally give each child a name. But too many elders had not survived the journey, and Minko's great-grandfather had been chosen to do the naming. The new names would signify some act of bravery or courage, or an outstanding character trait.

With their new names came privileges and the respect accorded to adults. Most boys did not receive their adult name until they had earned it, and that might not be until their fifteenth summer. Minko felt very important to be getting his new name in his eleventh summer. He knew he would soon have the right to go on the hunts with the men and the older boys. This was something he wanted more than anything.

"We have come together this day," Grandfather said to the crowd, "to honor the living and the dead. The families of these young men have spoken to me about brave deeds, extraordinary courage, and great hearts. They say that a name has been earned. It is an honor for me to give these young men those names today."

Laying his hands on the shoulders of the oldest boy, Grandfather said, "The name from your childhood is forgotten. You are now Strong Bull, so called for raising an overturned wagon by your strength alone, to save the life of a child."

"Thank you, Grandfather," said Strong Bull.

Grandfather called each boy forward, recognizing his deed and bestowing the new name. Minko was youngest, and last.

Grandfather smiled down at him and said, "From this day forward you will be Longwalker, so called for your strength and bravery on the dangerous walk to this place.

"This is a good day for all of us. Come forward then, young men, that we may greet you," Grandfather called in a loud voice. And one by one the people came and greeted the young men, calling them by their new names so that their ancestors would hear and remember them.

Longwalker stood, straight and proud, and greeted them all, accepting his new name and his new status in the tribe. He watched his father's face and saw the pride shining in his eyes. Then Itilakna's smile grew bigger, and his mother laughed out loud for the first time since she had arrived in Indian Territory.

What was so funny?

Then Longwalker heard the sound and knew the reason for the laughter. He turned around quickly and saw Black Spot racing toward him at full gallop. The young man was knocked

flat on his back as Black Spot plowed into him. He lay on the ground between the little pony's two front feet and looked up into the hairy face that was reaching down to snort softly into his chest. He started to laugh, and his laughter joined with that of his people and was carried away on the sweet spring air.

Author's Note

Longwalker was my great-great-grandfather. The family name of Walker began with the very next generation of the family, when Christian names were given to his children. He and his father, and a roguish Choctaw pony, really did walk to Indian Territory during the Choctaw removal, through one of the worst winter storms to hit Arkansas Territory in a hundred years.

I was a young girl when I first heard the story of Longwalker from my great-aunt, Myrtle Walker. She was the wife of my long-dead grandfather, Johnson Walker, who married Aunt Myrtle when her sister, my grandmother Minnie, died. The story is historically accurate, but a great many of the details had to be filled in because, sadly, most of the tale died with Aunt Myrtle. The scene where Minko Ushi plays hide-and-seek with Black Spot at the Memphis camp actually happened, as did the seven days Minko and Itilakna spent in a makeshift shelter. These are the only details that have survived in my memory over the past forty years.

Ulla Achufa Tok, which means "The Only Child," is my great-great-great-grandmother's real name. Itilakna, meaning "Yellow Tree," was my great-great-great-grandfather's name. But Longwalker's true childhood name has been lost, as well as his actual age during the walk. My aunt could only say that he was not yet twelve years old. I have called him Minko Ushi, which means "Little Chief." Black Spot is the name I gave the pony, based on the fact that he was said to be white with a black circle around one eye. The other characters in the story are fictitious, and the conversations came from my imagination. John Turner's family is representative of the many runaway slaves the Choctaws and other southeastern tribes aided during the early days of slavery.

The preservation of this story is very important to me. Although most of the details are gone forever, I know that my ancestors suffered terrible hardships and yet survived. I am living proof of that!

Acknowledgments

Without the resources of the Tulsa City County Library, it is very doubtful that this book could have been written. I am also indebted to the staff of the Choctaw Nation Museum in Mississippi for steering me in the right direction and suggesting two of the most invaluable books used in my research. These were *Indian Removal* (1953 ed.) by Grant Foreman, which contained some crucial maps, and *The Removal of the Choctaw Indians* by Arthur H. DeRosier, Jr. Other helpful material was found in *The Rise and Fall of the Choctaw Republic* by Angie Debo, and the Bureau of American Ethnology's publication #103, *Source Material for the Social and Ceremonial Life of the Choctaw Indians*.

    I would especially like to thank Charlie Jones, tribal historian and revered Choctaw elder, for his patience. He answered a million or so questions with unfailing kindness and meticulous accuracy.